The Queen

Also From Jennifer L. Armentrout

Fall With Me
Dream of You (a 1001 Dark Nights Novel)
Forever With You
Fire In You

By J. Lynn
Wait for You
Be With Me
Stay With Me

A Blood and Ash Novel
From Blood and Ash

The Covenant Series
Half-Blood
Pure
Deity
Elixer
Apollyon
Sentinel

The Lux Series
Shadows
Obsidian
Onyx
Opal
Origin
Opposition
Oblivion

The Origin Series
The Darkest Star
The Burning Shadow

The Dark Elements
Bitter Sweet Love
White Hot Kiss

Stone Cold Touch
Every Last Breath

The Harbinger Series
Storm and Fury
Rage and Ruin

A Titan Novel
The Return
The Power
The Struggle
The Prophecy

A Wicked Novel
Wicked
Torn
Brave
The Prince (a 1001 Dark Nights Novella)
The King (a 1001 Dark Nights Novella)
The Queen (a 1001 Dark Nights Novella)

Gamble Brothers Series
Tempting The Best Man
Tempting The Player
Tempting The Bodyguard

A de Vincent Novel Series
Moonlight Sins
Moonlight Seduction
Moonlight Scandals

Standalone Novels
Obsession
Frigid
Scorched
Cursed
Don't Look Back
The Dead List
Till Death

The Problem With Forever
If There's No Tomorrow

Anthologies
Meet Cute
Life Inside My Mind
Fifty First Times

The Queen

A Wicked Novella

By Jennifer L. Armentrout

1001 DARK NIGHTS
PRESS

The Queen
A Wicked Novella
By Jennifer L. Armentrout

1001 Dark Nights
Copyright 2020 Jennifer L. Armentrout
ISBN: 978-1-970077-61-2

Foreword: Copyright 2014 M. J. Rose

Published by 1001 Dark Nights Press, an imprint of Evil Eye Concepts, Incorporated

Acknowledgments from the Author

Thank you to Liz Berry, M.J. Rose, Jillian Stein, Chelle Olson, Kimberly Guidroz, and the amazing team behind 1001 Dark Nights for allowing me to tell Caden's and Brighton's story.

None of this would be possible without you, the reader. Thank you. Thank you.

Sign up for the 1001 Dark Nights Newsletter
and be entered to win a Tiffany Key necklace.

There's a contest every month!

Go to www.1001DarkNights.com to subscribe.

**As a bonus, all subscribers can download
FIVE FREE exclusive books!**

One Thousand and One Dark Nights

Once upon a time, in the future…

*I was a student fascinated with stories and learning.
I studied philosophy, poetry, history, the occult, and
the art and science of love and magic. I had a vast
library at my father's home and collected thousands
of volumes of fantastic tales.*

*I learned all about ancient races and bygone
times. About myths and legends and dreams of all
people through the millennium. And the more I read
the stronger my imagination grew until I discovered
that I was able to travel into the stories... to actually
become part of them.*

*I wish I could say that I listened to my teacher
and respected my gift, as I ought to have. If I had, I
would not be telling you this tale now.
But I was foolhardy and confused, showing off
with bravery.*

*One afternoon, curious about the myth of the
Arabian Nights, I traveled back to ancient Persia to
see for myself if it was true that every day Shahryar
(Persian: شهریار, "king") married a new virgin, and then
sent yesterday's wife to be beheaded. It was written
and I had read that by the time he met Scheherazade,
the vizier's daughter, he'd killed one thousand
women.*

Something went wrong with my efforts. I arrived in the midst of the story and somehow exchanged places with Scheherazade — a phenomena that had never occurred before and that still to this day, I cannot explain.

Now I am trapped in that ancient past. I have taken on Scheherazade's life and the only way I can protect myself and stay alive is to do what she did to protect herself and stay alive.

Every night the King calls for me and listens as I spin tales. And when the evening ends and dawn breaks, I stop at a point that leaves him breathless and yearning for more. And so the King spares my life for one more day, so that he might hear the rest of my dark tale.

As soon as I finish a story... I begin a new one... like the one that you, dear reader, have before you now.

Chapter 1

Pregnant.

Eight weeks pregnant. Maybe a little more.

The most common response in the history of womankind was dancing on the tip of my tongue, threatening to make me sound like an idiot.

That's not possible.

But the logical and sane voice in the back of my head whispered that it was as I stared at the silvery-skinned fae doctor. The same voice that also whispered, *that's what happens when you have unprotected sex, Brighton Jussier.*

That voice sounded a lot like my mother's during those moments when she had been herself and not the confused, lost shell of a woman the Winter fae attack had left behind.

"Are you okay?" Luce asked and then wrinkled her nose. "That's probably a stupid question. I doubt this was news you were expecting."

A strangled laugh escaped me. This wasn't even in the realm of things I'd expected. So many thoughts swirled as I sat on the plush couch of what could be considered a luxury suite in a place commonly referred to as Hotel Good Fae. Hidden by glamour, to human eyes, the building appeared to be a rundown and abandoned factory on South Peters Street, but the hotel was actually a stunning, massive community complex to all Summer fae who refused to feed on unwilling humans.

Right now, it felt like the entire building was made out of cardboard and could collapse at any second.

"How?" I whispered. "How is this possible?"

The blond fae who apparently worked part-time in a human clinic because, according to her, being intrigued by humans was similar to how wild animals fascinated zoologists, frowned. "Well, I imagine it happened during sex—"

"I know that." I cut her off. "But how could I survive being pregnant…after what I went through?" I couldn't even fathom how it was possible that a…pregnancy had survived the time I'd spent as Aric's captive. The psychotic Ancient fae who had killed my mother and left me for dead two years ago, had tortured me for weeks. For *months*. And it wasn't like I'd gotten three square meals a day.

"Your body has been through a lot," Luce repeated carefully. "Even for a fae, a viable pregnancy would be nothing short of a miracle. But for a human? It would be highly unlikely—"

"Then are you sure?"

"I cannot think of any other reason why you would have such an increase in that hormone. I want to do more testing. An ultrasound, for example. Some more blood work."

"I'm… I'm pregnant."

She gave a quick nod.

"Pregnant," I repeated, the information sort of sinking in. A child was growing inside me, right at this moment. I was… I was going to be a mother. My heart stuttered. Could I even be a mother? I was relatively organized and responsible. I was smart, and I'd had to take care of *my* mother from a very young age, but that was not the same thing as having to take care of a tiny human being. I had no idea what my future held.

Now my heart raced. Aric had…he'd fed from me repeatedly, just like the fae had done to my mother all those years ago. The trauma that had left her spontaneously going in and out of reality. I'd already had moments of being sucked into a world that seemed to exist only in my mind. There could be a chance I would wake up tomorrow and spend the entire day stuck in a world of terrifying memories and haunting hallucinations. I might spend days that way. Mom had sometimes spent weeks like that, and I…I didn't want to do that to a child. I knew what it felt like to see someone you loved, who was supposed to be the person that supported and took care of you, become trapped and unreachable. I wasn't bitter nor did I regret being there for my mom. Not at all. But when she was herself, I knew the knowledge that she needed constant care killed her.

I didn't want to repeat that cycle.

God, that was the last thing I wanted to do.

Luce's pale blue eyes searched mine. "It would help to know who the father is. That could possibly explain how this is likely."

I pulled myself from what felt like a downward spiral into flailing panic and drew in a tight, shallow breath.

Her shoulders squared as if she were preparing herself. "It is…obvious that the King cares for you deeply. When you were gone, he nearly tore the city of New Orleans apart looking for you. He's barely left your side since he found you, and sleeps only for a few hours here and there."

My heart squeezed painfully, and I closed my eyes. So much had happened since I woke up, no longer chained to what I believed would be my tomb. I'd just remembered what Aric had insinuated. That a Summer fae had been aiding him. I needed to tell Caden this. Not only that, I was still trying to process everything that had happened with Aric, what had come before that and after. And just an hour ago, I'd felt a sense of hope for the first time since Aric had taken me. The feeling had nearly stolen my breath.

Caden loved me. He'd ended his arranged engagement for me, but the awe-inspiring part was that I could still feel attraction and love after being trapped by Aric. The pain and the humiliation and the god-awful fear hadn't stolen the capability to desire, want, or love from me. Realizing that was life-altering. I knew that I could move on from what Aric had done, even if doing so took days or months or years. And I knew that Caden would be waiting for me, no matter how long it took.

That hope had crashed and burned spectacularly when Tatiana, the would-be Queen of the Summer Court, sat right where Luce was sitting now and explained what would happen if Caden didn't marry a fae of the Summer Court.

A King must choose a Queen to bear the next generation. Without doing so, the entire Summer Court would be weakened, and so would Caden. He would be dethroned, ostracized, and unprotected. Although he would no longer be a King, his blood still could be used by the Winter Court to commit unimaginable horror. Not only that, if what Tatiana claimed was true, the entire Court's fertility rate would continue to decrease until the entire race died out.

Caden must have known all of that when he ended the engagement with Tatiana. And while that was overwhelming in a way I had little experience with, it was also terrifying.

Because without the Summer fae fighting back against the Winter fae, mankind would fall. The Order I worked for wouldn't be able to hold them back.

It wasn't just the future of the Summer Court that relied on the King choosing his Queen. The entire world did as well.

I'd always dreamed about the kind of love where someone was willing to risk everything. I never thought I'd be on the receiving end of it, but I wanted it—wanted it so damn badly.

But was that kind of love worth everything? The downfall of the Summer Court? Mankind? I shuddered as the back of my nose burned. A part of me wanted to scream that yes it was, but could I really live with myself—live happily ever after for however long Caden and I had—while the world fell apart around us? Until the Winter Court came for him, and he wasn't able to fight them off?

Could Caden really live with that?

He might think so now, but months and years from now? I didn't think so.

I knew I couldn't.

And now, with the knowledge that I could...that I *was* bringing a child into a world that would definitely have an expiration date stamped on it? I couldn't do that.

Luce had tipped forward when I reopened my damp eyes. "Is it possible, Brighton, that the King is the father? Or could it be someone else?"

"Aric didn't...he didn't rape me."

"You said you didn't remember anything like that," she clarified gently. "I would think it would be unlikely for it to be him, based on the stage of your pregnancy. But if it happened at the beginning of your captivity, it wouldn't be wholly *im*possible."

I was pretty sure Aric hadn't forced himself on me. To be honest, he'd seemed pretty disgusted by humans, especially me. But toward the end, I'd thought he started to respect me, as messed up as that was. If I hadn't been able to kill him when I did, I had a horrible, sinking feeling that this conversation might be different.

I shook my head. "It's not him."

Luce's gaze met mine. "Then the King is the father. Or possibly someone else?"

The breath I exhaled punched out of me. "There's no one else. It has to be him. We had...well, we were together, and there wasn't protection. I didn't think it would be a concern."

Luce didn't move for several moments. I wasn't even sure if she breathed, but then she swallowed and sat up straight. "It's extremely rare for a human to become pregnant by a fae, but it happens."

I knew that. A halfling could be born from such a union. Ivy Owens was a prime example of that—

"The prophecy." I jolted, heart leaping into my throat. "The one that could cause the gates of the Otherworld to open—"

"You're not a halfling," Luce interceded calmly. "Your child most likely wouldn't even be one."

Yes, she was right. The prophecy that would tear open the gates between our worlds, freeing the demented Queen Morgana, required a Prince or Princess or a King or Queen to procreate with a halfling, creating a child that should never exist. I knew that. I wasn't a halfling, but I also wasn't exactly human anymore, was I? The King had given me the Summer Kiss, something that no one else knew. Well, no one who was alive. Aric had figured it out, but—

"Wait." My brain had finally processed everything she'd said. "M-my child most likely wouldn't be a halfling? It would be human?"

"No." Luce leaned forward again, pressing the tips of her fingers together. "The child would most likely be completely fae."

I opened my mouth, closed it, and then tried again. "How is that even possible? I'm human." Mostly. "And he is fae. His genetics can't cancel out mine."

"Actually, for the King or for an Ancient, they would."

I stared at her. "Does science mean nothing to you people?"

A faint smile appeared. "Only to a certain degree, Brighton. We are not human, and we are not bound by human science, biology, or genetics. We are far more superior than that." A pause. "No offense meant."

I blinked at her.

"This could explain why the pregnancy is still viable despite the trauma to your body," Luce went on, a look of curiosity creeping across her face. "A child of a King would be incredibly strong, even at this stage and inside a human incubator."

"Human incubator?" I repeated. "Can you please never refer to me as that again?"

"Sorry." She dipped her chin. "I know you are more than that. Sometimes my mind is far too…clinical for the comfort of others."

"Really?" I said dryly.

Seeming to miss my sarcasm, she nodded. "The King being the father lessens some of my concerns over what risks you'll face. I would even be willing to suggest that the pregnancy might continue to be viable."

Viable.

I was beginning to dislike that word. I looked down, realizing I was still wearing the fluffy white robe. "What...? I mean, will this pregnancy be different from a normal one?"

Luce appeared to think that over. "It's hard to say. Not many Ancients have impregnated a human before. But I can tell you what a pregnancy for a fae is like."

Unsure if I really wanted to know, I nodded anyway.

"Pregnancy terms are about the same as humans. Nine months. Not many fae are born prematurely without there being a physical cause, like an injury," she explained. "Most fae only experience sickness during the first two or so months."

The vomiting spells were suddenly brought to a whole new light. I'd thought it had been the trauma and my stomach adjusting to food.

"The threat of miscarriage also usually only exists in the first two to three months," she went on. "We are extremely lucky compared to human women in that sense."

Yes, they were.

"The progression of the fetus is relatively the same as it is for a human." Luce loosely clasped her hands together. "Come to think of it, our pregnancies are rather uneventful compared to humans'. I imagine yours will be too."

I slowly became unaware that my hand was pressed to my lower stomach. I hadn't realized that I'd even placed it there. My stomach felt flat—flatter than it had ever been.

Luce studied me like I was some strange creature she'd never come into contact with before. "You're handling the news well."

"I am?" A brittle laugh parted my lips. "I think it's because none of this seems real, and I... after what I've gone through? I don't know. I don't think I've truly processed any of this." My gaze shifted to the closed door. "It's not like there's anything I can do about it."

"There are options, Brighton."

My head jerked back to her.

"The same ones available to human women," she added quietly.

Shock flickered through me. Not because of what she was suggesting. I was relieved to hear that fae women had a choice, but I was stunned that she would even bring it up, considering who the father was.

But then I thought of how her face had paled when she first asked if the King could be the father. "What will happen if the King doesn't take a Queen?"

The only visible reaction was the tension around Luce's mouth. "He would be dethroned, and since he's ascended to the throne already, his brother would not be able to take it. We would be without a King."

"And the entire Court would fail—would become vulnerable to the Winter fae," I said.

Luce inhaled sharply through her nose and then nodded. "It would be very…catastrophic for all if that were to happen."

Tatiana hadn't lied.

Then again, I hadn't thought she had.

"Is that why you're telling me I have options?" I asked, knowing that Luce had no idea that Caden had already ended his engagement with Tatiana. "Because the child and I might get in the way of Caden marrying a fae?"

Her eyes widened slightly. "I'm letting you know you have options because, as a healer that is my duty. What I personally feel has no bearing on what you decide to do."

I believed her. Luce seemed too, as she said, clinical "But do you think it will get in the way?"

"What I think is not a part of my duty, Brighton."

"But what is happening could impact your future," I persisted.

She looked away, lips pressing into a flat line. She was quiet for so long that I didn't think she was going to answer. "I believe that our King knows how important it is to the entire Court. He will not fail us."

My heart did a weird thing. It swelled because even knowing how important his duty was, the King had chosen *me*. Then it sank all the way to the pit of my stomach because he was going to fail them.

Her gaze slid back to mine. "Tatiana was here before I arrived. I imagine she has become more than aware of the King's feelings for you. I do not believe he has spent more than a handful of minutes with her. I also imagine it was she who filled you in on what would happen if the King doesn't choose a Queen."

Seeing no point in lying, I nodded.

"Did she tell you that while some fae choose to be monogamous, we are accepting of relationships which do not start with one person and end with a second. Especially for someone like our King, whose duties may not align with his heart."

"She did, but…" My mind was all over the place. "But you're suggesting that Caden could marry a fae while keeping me and…and our child in the picture?"

"Yes. However, he would also need to provide an heir," she said. Before I could question that, she added, "I'm sure your child with him will be a full-blooded fae, but only a child between the King and Queen would be recognized as a Prince or Princess."

"This is some medieval bullshit nonsense," I told her.

She lifted her hands helplessly. "Be that as it may, would that kind of arrangement be suitable to you?"

"Basically, being a mistress with a child that wouldn't be recognized—"

"I am sure your son or daughter would be welcomed warmly and would be loved and taken care of," she interceded. "We are not *that* medieval."

Never in my life did I think to even answer a question like this. "No," I said, and it rang true. "It's not like I think unorthodox relationships are wrong. I couldn't care less. It's just not something I could do. I couldn't even try."

Luce opened her mouth and then closed it. Several moments passed. "You don't have to decide anything right now."

"But I do." I closed my eyes briefly. "I mean, I already have. I will keep the b-baby." I rose swiftly on unsteady legs, causing Luce's gaze to turn wary. "I'm pro-choice and pro-mind your-own-business. But I can't do that."

And I couldn't.

I looked down at the fluffy robe as a knot of raw emotion choked me. I was pregnant. This was my child. This was Caden's child. *Our* child. And he or she would be the only thing I would have of Caden. A small, beautiful piece of him. Proof that our love for one another was real, even if we hadn't the chance to explore it.

Because I could not risk the world.

Not even for love.

Chapter 2

Luce watched me as if she expected me to topple over at any second, which was possible. As I started to pace in front of the couch, I felt as if each step were as uncertain as a child learning to walk.

Something that I would have to help this child learn.

Oh God.

I would need to teach the child how to eat, brush their teeth, sit up, and—

"So, what are you going to do then?" Luce asked.

That was a good question. What *was* I going to do? Who could I even ask? I had very few friends, and none of them had any baby-making experience. But I knew I couldn't stay. Leaving here would be hard. I'd never been anywhere before, but I would have to move. Where? No clue. I felt pretty confident that the Order would approve a transfer, especially after everything that had happened. Then what? I'd be a single mother to a full-blooded fae?

A single mom who may or may not lose control of her senses?

That would be problematic.

Rubbing my brow, I continued pacing. "I don't know exactly what I'm doing, but I can't...I can't stay here."

Her brows lifted. "During your pregnancy? I imagine that the King would want you to stay with him—"

"Caden can't know." I stopped walking and lowered my hand.

Luce blinked once and then twice. "You're not planning to tell him?"

My heart thumped against my chest. "No. I can't."

"Do you think he wouldn't be receptive to news of a child? I don't know him well at all—"

"No. It's not that." Honestly, I had no idea if he would be amenable or not. It wasn't like we'd had a chance to talk about any of this.

She frowned. "I know this is shocking news, and on top of everything else. You have to be experiencing a lot of confusion."

I was definitely feeling a decent amount of confusion, but I knew one thing for sure. Caden couldn't know. "I'm not confused about this. He can't know. You're just like a human doctor. You told me that what I say to you and what my condition is stays between us. You won't tell Caden."

"I would never betray a patient's trust by doing so, but I also won't betray my King," she stated, and pressure clamped down on my chest. "You want me to hide his child from him?"

The judgment and disbelief in her tone were evident. "You just said what you feel has no bearing," I reminded her. "And you're obviously feeling something right now."

"You're right." Luce rose with the grace of a trained dancer. "But if you're planning to keep this child, bring him or her into this world, you cannot expect me to keep that from the King."

"But you would keep an abortion from him?" I challenged.

"I never said that."

My mouth dropped open. "I don't think you understand what patient-doctor confidentiality means."

"And I don't think *you* understand what being the subject of a King means."

She was right. I didn't. But that didn't change anything. I needed to convince her to keep her mouth shut, and that wasn't easy when I honestly had no idea what I was going to do. "Just give me a moment. I need to think."

"You need to take more than a couple of moments, Brighton."

I pinched the bridge of my nose as I raced over the possible options like I did when I mapped out the best possible routes for Order members to take when they were needed. "I don't plan to keep the child from him forever. I wouldn't do that," I decided, and that was true. "That wouldn't be fair to Caden or the child."

"I'm relieved to hear that." She crossed her arms. "But that's very contrary to stating that he cannot know."

"He just can't know right now."

"Brighton—"

"You don't understand, Luce. He can't know right now. Okay? I will tell him, but not now."

"When will you?"

"When the time is right."

Luce stared back at me, and then her gaze lowered as she nodded. "All right."

Instinct flared. I knew she was lying. Everything in me said so. She may not go straight to Caden, but she would whenever I passed whatever time limit she set. I was angry that there was really no confidentiality here, but I also understood that I had no grasp of what it meant to have a King or to be fae. Human norms couldn't be expected. I still needed to stop her, and I only knew of one way.

"He's already ended his engagement," I told her.

"What?" Her gaze sharpened.

"He already ended his betrothal to Tatiana." I sat down, suddenly so very tired. "He…he chose me. Only me." My voice cracked as I scrubbed my palms down my face. "He's already made his choice."

Luce stumbled back a step and then plopped into the chair. Any other time, I would've laughed at seeing a fae being so ungraceful, but there was nothing funny here. She understood what I was saying.

"Tatiana told me. That was why she came here. She didn't come out of jealousy. At least it didn't appear that way to me. She was even open to me being a part of his life so long as he married a fae—any fae." Tears blurred my eyes. "No one else knows. Caden wasn't going to announce it until after Tatiana had left."

Her lips parted.

"I knew then that I…I couldn't let him do this. I love him—" I sucked in a sharp, burning breath. "I want him. I want to be his only choice. But I can't be the reason the entire world goes to hell."

Luce said nothing.

"The moment what Tatiana said sank in, I knew I had to…I don't know, make him think that I didn't want to be with him or something. I knew that I needed to leave." I brushed a fat tear off my cheek. "Having his child can't change that. It can't, Luce. And I really don't think him learning that he's about to become a father is going to push him in the right direction."

She remained silent.

I took another breath that went nowhere. "So, once he c-chooses his Queen and is married, then I can tell him about the child. I swear I will. Because, like I said, it wouldn't be fair to the child or to him." My heart felt like it was cracking and splintering. "I didn't want to say anything, but you have to understand why he can't know right now. Please tell me you understand."

Luce stared at me.

Seconds ticked away, and I started to worry. I sat back. "Are you...are you okay?"

Finally, she moved—well, she blinked, but that was definitely better than sitting there and staring at me. Then she spoke in a voice barely above a whisper. "You're his *mortuus*."

My heart skipped a beat. I was Caden's *mortuus*. His heart, his everything, and his greatest weakness. Through me, all manner of things could be done to Caden. Aric had only realized what I was when he figured out that Caden had given me the Summer Kiss. "Why would you say that?"

"It's the only reason he would be willing to forsake his entire Court." Luce lifted a trembling hand, smoothing down hair that was already pin-straight. "That goes beyond love, beyond what most of us can even fathom." Awe filled her pale eyes. "It's a connection of two souls and two hearts. It's rare for any fae to find their *mortuus*, but to do so with a human? I..." She trailed off and then gave herself a little shake. The shock cleared from her face. "No one can know what you are to him. That kind of information is far too dangerous. You're safe here, but if it were to get out—"

"I know." Aric could've told Neal, who was still somewhere out there. And if someone from the Summer Court was aiding him, he could've told them. Aric might have told me that he told them. Perhaps I simply didn't remember. The feedings...

I pulled myself out of those thoughts.

Luce was now really staring at me, like I was some sort of new creature. "Fate can be so cruel sometimes."

"It really can," I whispered.

She lowered her gaze, falling silent.

"Am I wrong?" I asked, genuinely curious. "Am I wrong to walk away from him? To keep this from him until he marries?"

"No, you're doing the right thing." She rose and then sat beside me. A jolt of surprise went through me as she picked up my hand. "You are quite admirable, Brighton. More than most fae could ever be. You've survived what I am sure many have succumbed to—too many to count. And to put my people before your own needs, to sacrifice what you must feel for the King for people who will never know what you were willing to give up? That makes you as brave as any warrior, if not more."

Speechless, I blinked back tears. I didn't think she knew what that meant. So many people didn't. They didn't believe in my competencies or strength, that I was capable of acts of bravery. The Order didn't. Not even Miles, who ran it. It took me getting captured and surviving for even Ivy to realize that I was no longer the quiet, shy Brighton who was only good for research.

Luce squeezed my hand and said, "I won't say anything, and I will help you in whatever way I can. But, Brighton, I must be honest."

I tensed.

"I don't know if it will be enough. I fear that what is done is done."

Unease blossomed. "What do you mean?"

Her gaze locked onto mine. "I don't think you'll be able to walk away from the King. That there will be anything that you can do to cause him to choose a Queen that is not you. You're his *mortuus*, the other half of his soul, his heart. And it is very unlikely that he'll give you up. Ever."

Chapter 3

After a drawn-out battle of wills between Luce and I, she promised not to protest my leaving Hotel Good Fae as long as I agreed to stay for the remainder of the week for observation and met her at the clinic she worked at next week for an ultrasound and bloodwork. Since it was Monday, that meant five days before I could go home. Five days where I would be in the same building with the man I loved but couldn't have.

I wasn't exactly happy, but I relented. My body had been through a lot. So had my mind, and with the latest development, I needed to be somewhere Luce could easily check in on me.

Relief that she was going to stay quiet overshadowed the irritation of being stuck here. But what she'd said sat heavily on my chest as I pulled on a pair of loose sweats and a shirt Ivy had left for me.

Could Luce be right? Caden would never let me go?

My hands shook as I pulled my hair back into a ponytail. Part of me was thrilled to hear that Luce believed Caden felt that strongly for me. That he wouldn't let me push him away. That was the incredibly selfish part of me that was doing jumping jacks at the prospect of Caden fighting for me. For us. The other half was terrified over what was at stake.

Stopping in the middle of the room, I looked down. *I'm pregnant.* A wave of shivers skittered over my skin. Hands still trembling, I reached down and lifted my shirt. I tried to see past the way my stomach caved in and the old, pale scars left behind from Aric's first attack as well as the fresher, angry red cuts that covered nearly every inch of my midsection. There was a…a baby in there, right now, *growing.* My child.

Our child.

A wealth of emotions rose, so many that I could barely decipher the unexpected excitement from all the fear of the unknown and what needed to be done.

If things were different, I would still be scared out of my mind. I never really thought hard about having children. I'd had to take care of my mom, and then there had been my need for revenge. There hadn't been any serious relationships in the last several years. It just hadn't been something I thought about. So, I would still be afraid. I'd be wondering if I was capable of caring for a baby. I would still have no idea if I'd be a good mother. But that burst of excitement I'd felt a few seconds before wouldn't have been squashed by all the fear. It would continue to grow, and maybe some of that trepidation would lessen over time. Instead of thinking about how I was going to make Caden understand that he had to be with someone else, I would be obsessing over how to break the news. I wouldn't be trying to figure out how to leave, or where I could go. I would be worrying about normal things like how Caden would take the news. Would he be happy? Scared? Disappointed? If things were different, I wouldn't be spending one moment hiding the pregnancy from him.

God, that hurt. I hated the whole idea of hiding it. That wasn't who I was. But things weren't different. I was pragmatic enough to realize that these were the cards I had been dealt, and it didn't matter how unfair that hand was.

I pressed my palm against the skin of my stomach, wincing as the many slices stung. Here were the facts: I was pregnant with the King of the Summer Court's child. He loved me, and I loved him. But the fate of the actual world rested on him choosing a Queen from his people. I knew I didn't have it in me to share him, even if he married someone and eventually slept with them only out of duty. I couldn't do it. We had to put the world before ourselves, and I needed to somehow get Caden to see that. More importantly, there were more immediate, pressing concerns. Aric was dead, but Neal was still out there. He may not be as powerful or as smart as Aric, but I didn't think he'd tuck tail and run like Caden thought he would. Even if he did, there was still the issue of someone within the Summer Court working with the Winter fae. I needed to find Caden and tell him what I'd remembered. I had to do that before I even tried to talk some sense into him or find a way to get him to do the right thing.

Letting go of my shirt, I watched the soft fabric flutter back into place. It was then I realized that I was crying. I wiped at my cheeks a little too roughly. It hurt the still-healing bruises.

"Pull it together," I said, forcing myself to take a deep breath. "You need to pull it together, Bri."

And I did. It took a while, but I was able to do what I'd done while being held captive by Aric. I shut my emotions down and locked them away. Only then did I toe on a pair of flip-flops Ivy had brought and leave the room.

The hall to the elevator was blessedly empty. I stepped inside, hitting the button for the first floor. I had no idea which room Caden was staying in, but if he was up and moving about, I figured he'd either be in or near Tanner's office. If not, Tanner could probably tell me where he was. I rode the elevator down, not letting myself think of anything.

A mysterious sugary scent hit me the moment the elevator doors opened to the wide hall that split in three different directions. My stomach grumbled. There was a bakery in the cafeteria area, and they must've put out a fresh batch of something. With great effort, I forced myself to turn right instead of walking straight toward the cafeteria. I headed down the brightly lit hall. Reaching the corner—

I came face-to-face with several silvery-skinned fae. I didn't recognize any of them, but there was no mistaking the shock on their faces as they got an eyeful of me. I had no idea if they knew who I was, but it was obvious that they saw someone who looked as if they had gone toe-to-toe with a professional boxer and lost. My left eye was open, but it was more purple than pink, and the lid felt incredibly heavy. The swelling had reduced a little along my cheek, but I still looked like I had food shoved in there. The cut in my bottom lip didn't nearly look as bad as it had this morning, but it was still angry-looking.

Then there was the band of bruised skin around my neck.

One of the fae, a younger male, stared at that, and I realized I probably should've left my hair down. Or found a turtleneck. And a ski mask.

They hurried around me, saying nothing, and I trudged on, seeing the open door to Tanner's office up ahead. Above me, one of the recessed lights flickered—

Say it!

I jerked to a stop, air lodging in my throat as Aric's voice thundered in my ears and all around me. He wasn't here. I knew that. He was dead, and I wasn't in that awful place. I was safe. I'd killed him. I was—

Say it!

Clapping my hands over my ears, I tried to silence the roar of Aric's voice, but the hallway around me darkened. The walls became damp, moldy bricks. I inhaled sharply, no longer smelling sugar but mold and decay. Blood. I staggered forward. *Chains clinked.* The weight unbearable around my neck. *I'm not there. I'm not there.* The floor shifted under my feet, and I felt my knees connect with the stone, but the pain barely registered. Aric's cold breath was against my cheek.

"Say it," he demanded, his voice echoing around me, through me. "Say please."

"No. No. No," I whispered, doubling over.

Hands touched my shoulders, and I jerked back, expecting biting pain to follow. I couldn't take anymore. I couldn't—

A voice broke through the haze of panic, a timbre that was deep and smooth. Comforting. I thought I recognized it. Whoever it was said something. A name. *Brighton.* More words. *Open your eyes.* My fingers curled into the hair above my ears. I'd heard those words before. *Open your eyes, sunshine.*

Sunshine.

That…that meant something. Meaning was attached to that. Emotions. Happiness. Sadness. Safety.

Arms shifted around me, and I felt as if I were floating for several seconds before being settled against something warm and hard. It moved. Rose up and down steadily against the side of my body as a voice whispered, "It's okay. I'm here. I've got you. I've always got you."

Fingers curled around my wrists. They were warm, not at all like Aric's. His skin was ice cold. I focused on the feeling of those fingers as they slowly pulled mine away from my ears. This wasn't Aric. He was dead. I'd killed him. I wasn't there. I knew that. My arms were lowered to my lap. I didn't want to look because I had the distinct feeling that I'd heard this all before. And once…once it hadn't been real.

What if none of this was real?

Maybe I was still in that cold, damp, and dark place, chained to the stone slab. My heart stuttered as a hoarse sound crawled up and out of me.

Those warm fingers touched my right cheek, and I started to draw back, but a gentle touch followed. "Open your eyes for me." The voice came again. "Please open your eyes so you can see me and know that it's me holding you, touching you. That you're safe. Open your eyes, sunshine."

I did, and I found myself looking into two amber jewels. Not Aric's icy eyes. Not the pale blue of a normal fae. Hot, golden eyes thickly fringed with heavy lashes. My gaze moved over the straight, proud nose and the full, expressive lips, to the sculpted jaw and blond strands of hair that rested against high, sharp cheekbones.

He cupped my cheeks, careful not to put pressure on the left side of my face as he guided my gaze back to his. "Your name is Brighton Jussier. Your friends sometimes call you Bri. Tink calls you Lite Bright," he said, those beautiful eyes searching mine. "I call you my sunshine. Do you know why? It's because I saw you smile once, and it was like the sun finally rising after centuries of nothing but night."

A deep shudder started inside me and then rippled out over my skin. With the next breath I took, the scent of summer rain and long, hot nights surrounded me.

It was like waking up from a nightmare with your eyes already open. I was stuck somewhere, and then I was here.

I knew who I was.

I knew where I was.

And I also knew who held me.

The King.

Caden.

Chapter 4

Impossibly, all thoughts fled the moment Caden smiled.

He was a stunning man, but when those full lips curved into a grin, he became breathtakingly beautiful. Everything that had led to this moment took a backseat. It was just Caden and me, his warm body against mine, and his hands ever so gently holding me.

I'm carrying his child.

I didn't know who moved first. If it was him. If it was me. Or both of us. What mattered was that our lips met. My breath snagged. He was more than aware of the cut along my lower lip, knew just the right pressure so it wouldn't cause even a second of pain. And it felt like a first kiss. In a way, it was. Our last kiss like this had been weeks ago—months ago. An eternity. Before Aric, before things I knew were important but couldn't pull from my scattered thoughts.

There was no thinking. Only sensation as I felt as if I sank into him. Caden was so incredibly careful, avoiding the numerous areas of aches and pains. He sipped from my lips in slow, drugging kisses that sent a flush of heady warmth through my body, chasing away the iciness of what had just occurred.

He tasted rich and lush as one of his hands lowered to my hip. I could feel the tension in his lax grip, as if he wanted to grab me, hold me tight but held back.

Caden and the kiss…they were both so incredibly gentle, so *loving*. A swelling motion rose in my heart, and a rawness appeared in my soul. I no longer had to fantasize about how it felt to be kissed by someone who didn't just love me but also cherished me. Because that was how I was kissed right then. It was one of the most beautiful and painful realizations.

All those scattered thoughts were piecing themselves together, reminding me of what exactly had just happened and everything that had come before.

I shouldn't be doing this—allowing this. Too much was at stake. I needed to distance myself from Caden. Not make out with him.

Caden ended the kiss before I had the common sense to do so. He pulled away just enough that his forehead rested on mine. Against my arm, I could feel his strong heart pounding. "I missed that little catch in your breath," he murmured. "I missed the taste of you on my tongue."

Heat swamped me, and I wanted to let it drown me. Then I wouldn't care about the consequences.

God.

I shouldn't have let him kiss me.

Or I shouldn't have kissed him.

My lips still tingled. Other parts of me were also doing that, and I didn't need the reminder to make what I had to do even harder. I had to put as much space between us as I could, but my body and heart had different ideas. I tipped forward, resting my unbruised cheek on his shoulder. There was no hesitation from Caden. His arms swept around me, and a sigh I couldn't hope to hide parted my lips. He held me so very carefully, mindful of all the hurts. In his arms, I felt as if nothing could reach me—not the past or the future, not even the horrible dread that I would become just like my mom, or the knowledge that I had to walk away from Caden. I felt cherished and protected. Safe.

Caden drew a hand over my head, down the loose ponytail, and then over the line of my spine. The steady sweep of his hand was soothing. I didn't know how much time passed as I soaked up his warmth, his closeness, but then he spoke. "I just missed you, Brighton."

My heart squeezed as if a hand reached inside and gripped it, and all that warmth from before was chased away by cold, harsh reality.

Caden lifted his head then, his gaze coasting over my features as if they were flawless. He smiled again, but I realized it didn't quite reach his eyes. A wealth of concern rested there, and I hated seeing that. "How are you feeling now?"

I dragged my gaze from his, focusing on the patch of golden skin above the collar of his black shirt. "I feel okay."

"Truly?"

I nodded, having a feeling that he knew better.

"I have a lot of questions."

Not exactly surprising.

"Starting with the most important one," he continued. "What are you doing out of bed?"

I blinked. That was the most important thing? He'd found me in a hallway, having what was definitely a hallucination, and he was asking why I was out of bed? I started to move, reminding myself that we definitely needed space between us, but the hand at my back held me in place.

I didn't fight him. I could've, and I believed if I pushed, he'd let go, but I didn't. *Just a little longer*, I told myself. "I was looking for you," I admitted.

"Flattered," he murmured, smoothing down the wisps of my hair with his other hand. "But you should be resting and taking it easy. Neither of those two things includes roaming around the hotel."

"I wasn't roaming around." I looked up at him. "And I feel fine."

Caden stared at me.

I sighed. "I mean, I physically feel okay."

He sat back a little, and I realized we were in one of the meeting rooms near Tanner's office, sitting on a couch. Well, he was sitting on the couch. I was sitting on him, my legs resting on the cushion next to us. "You want to tell me what happened out there?"

Not really, but he'd seen me worse than this. When he found me in that underground chamber, I had been much harder to reach. "I don't know what happened. I was coming down to tell you something, and one of the ceiling lights flickered." My nose scrunched as I looked away again, focusing on a bouquet of purplish-pink irises. "Actually, I'm not even sure if the light flickered or not."

"They did in Tanner's office. A power surge, I believe," he said.

Knowing I hadn't hallucinated that part brought forth a small measure of relief. "After I saw the light, I..."

"What?" he asked softly.

My cheeks heated. "I heard Aric's voice." Aware that the movement of his hand had halted at the mention of the Winter fae, I forced myself to keep talking. "I knew he wasn't here, but it was like being sucked into this...this hallucination. I don't know if the light triggered it or what. With Mom, I don't think there was anything in particular that caused her to lose the sense of who she was. But I couldn't pull myself out of it. And I...I knew who I was." A shiver worked its way through me. "Mom always did, but it was like I didn't know where I was or what was real. I can't..." I exhaled roughly as I gave a little shake of my head. "It wasn't the first time I'd heard his voice or hallucinated. When I was there, I thought I saw a lot of things. And with Mom, it wasn't as bad when she first came back. But it steadily got worse."

Caden's hand started moving again. "I know you're aware of this. Too many feedings can fracture a human's mind. It doesn't take much."

I did know that. Even if I hadn't seen it firsthand with my mom, I could see it every day on the streets of New Orleans. Humans who stumbled around mindlessly, some easily mistaken for addicts while others became uncontrollable, violent creatures. It also happened when a fae bent human minds to their will too often.

"I know you're afraid that you're going to become your mom, but you're stronger than that."

"Mom was the strongest woman I knew."

"I don't know that, but you're different. You're not entirely human," Caden said quietly. Slowly, my gaze lifted to his. The Summer Kiss. "You're going to heal from this. All the bruises and the cuts will heal. Your mind will heal. You just need time. And you have time."

God, I wanted to latch on to that and believe him, but I wasn't sure if he was telling me that so I'd have hope, or if he was being truthful. But I really didn't have time. There were important things to deal with.

Namely one that would be arriving in roughly seven months—give or take a week.

Pressure settled on my shoulders, and I had to change the subject. If not, I was likely to blurt out everything.

"What is it?" he asked, curling his fingers around my chin. He guided my gaze back to his.

My heart tripped over itself. "What do you mean?"

"Something is bothering you," he said. "Something that's not about what just happened. What are you not telling me?"

Panic flared in the pit of my stomach as my throat dried, and it became difficult to swallow.

"You're scared. That, I understand." His thumb swept over the curve of my chin. "But there's sadness there too. I can feel it drenching your skin. You've been through a lot. I know, but this is different. You weren't like this when I left you earlier or any other time."

I froze. He couldn't know. Caden could sense emotions, which meant hiding anything from him was difficult, but he wasn't a mind reader. There was no way.

My mind rapidly searched for an explanation. Luckily, I remembered why I'd set out in search of him. If what Aric claimed was true, that would give me a reason to be sad. I latched on to that and ran with it. "It's what I came down to tell you. I remembered—"

A soft knock on the door interrupted me, followed by Tanner's voice. "My King? Is everything all right?"

Caden's gaze didn't leave me as he all but growled, "Everything's fine. I'll be in to see you when I can."

"Wait!" I shouted, scrambling out of Caden's lap. He frowned, but I ignored that and the flare of pain that shot through my body.

"I'm…I'm waiting," came Tanner's tentative response through the door.

"We're not done talking," Caden told me.

"This involves him." And it did. Also, I seriously doubted that Caden would pursue his earlier questioning while Tanner was present. The older fae was also the perfect buffer. "Please come in."

The door didn't open. Confused, I looked at Caden, who sighed. "It's okay," he announced, draping an arm along the back of the couch. "You may come in, Tanner."

My brows lifted. "Really?"

He winked. "I'm the King."

"Whatever," I muttered as the door opened.

Tanner entered, dressed as if he were about to go out for a round of golf. Beige, pressed trousers and a light blue polo shirt, wrinkle-free. All he was missing was a glove. He couldn't look more…human. The silvery hair at his temples was spreading, proof that he didn't feed from humans. Sometimes I wondered if my mom had developed a bit of a crush on Tanner, one that had been reciprocated. Mom liked him, so I trusted Tanner.

He wasn't alone.

A dark-haired fae followed him in. Faye's silvery skin was darker than Tanner's, often reminding me of a stunning pewter shade. While Faye had the most impressive resting bitch face I'd ever seen, and I often wasn't sure if she actually liked me, she had a no-nonsense mentality, and I trusted her. She, like Kalen, another fae, were warriors. They didn't feed on humans, so they could be killed a lot easier than those who did, but they were still faster and stronger than any human could ever hope to be.

Faye's cousin Benji was one of the missing younglings, and I suspected that he wouldn't be returning to the hotel. There was a good chance that he, like the others, had somehow gotten ahold of Devil's Breath, a liquor laced with a drug derived from the *borrachero* tree. It turned humans into virtual zombies, and the fae into evil creatures controlled by the Winter fae.

"We're sorry to interrupt," Tanner said, clasping his hands behind him as he glanced over at me. "We were just worried."

"We heard you shout in the hall," Faye explained.

Well, that explained how Caden had found me. "I'm fine."

Faye lifted a dark brow. "You don't look fine."

I couldn't be offended by Faye's bluntness. "I feel better than I look."

"I would hope," Tanner murmured.

Faye walked to where I stood, her gaze coasting over my face. My muscles stiffened as I forced myself not to flinch or take a step back. It had nothing to do with Faye, but with the fact that Aric had been really good at teaching me to be wary of anyone getting too close. Oddly aware of the tension radiating off Caden, I held myself still as she placed a hand on my shoulder. "I heard that it was you who killed Aric."

"It was."

Her eyes glimmered. "The next time I need backup, I know who to call."

Pride swept through me like golden fire. Out of everyone, Faye never doubted my ability to fight and defend myself, even though she saw my thirst for revenge as a risk. She hadn't just seen me as the *Willow* to the *Buffy*, something that had taken a while for Ivy to recognize.

"I'm not sure how I feel about that," Caden said.

"It's a good thing you don't have a say in what I do," I retorted.

Tanner's eyes widened while the glimmer in Faye's deepened.

"But I do have a say in what she does," Caden remarked.

I shot him a look, to which he simply grinned. Then I remembered what Caden had told me. Ivy and Faye had helped to change my bandages while I was unconscious. "Thank you for helping to take care of me."

She inclined her head. "You would do the same for me, would you not?"

"Of course."

"Because that's what friends do for one another, even human and fae friends," she said, and a hint of a smile pulled at her lips when I rolled my eyes. "More importantly, that's what warriors do for one another."

Warriors.

She was talking about *me*.

Twice in one day, someone had referred to me as a warrior. I liked that. A lot.

Tanner replaced Faye and took my hands in his. "I am relieved to see you here. We didn't lose hope that you would be returned, but that hope didn't lessen our fears. After what happened to you and…and Merle, I couldn't…" He trailed off, lips tightening in a grimace as he cleared his throat.

A ball formed in the back of my throat as I squeezed his hands. "I know."

His pale eyes searched mine. "I am relieved to see you up and moving about, but are you sure you're ready for that?"

"You know," Caden began as Tanner let go of my hands, "I was saying just the same thing to her."

"I'm ready. Besides, I think getting up and moving around will help with the whole healing thing. Anyway," I cut in before Caden could reply. "I hope I didn't interrupt your meeting,"

Tanner appeared as if he wished to say that I had, but he seemed to know better than to say that in front of Caden. "Not at all." His lie was so smooth, it brought a faint smile to my face. I knew that Tanner liked me—well, liked me when I wasn't calling Caden names. But I also suspected that he would not be pleased to learn that there was a relationship between Caden and me. Then again, I imagined he already knew that something was going on. "We were discussing a few important details—"

"That can easily be discussed later," Caden interjected. I had a feeling it was about Caden's impending engagement. I doubted that Tanner knew it had been canceled.

The male fae nodded. "Of course."

"I'm actually glad you guys came by," I said, moving so I sat on the chair across from a square ottoman. Caden's head tilted to the side as he watched me. "I remembered something that Aric said—something I think you all need to know."

Tanner sat in the other chair, and Faye moved to stand behind him. "What is it?"

"I wish I'd remembered this sooner," I said, almost apologetically. "But things have been..." *Kind of a mess in my head?* I didn't say that.

"It's okay. I understand," Caden said. "They understand."

I lowered my gaze and took a deep, steady breath, clearing my thoughts. "Aric said that someone within the Summer Court has been helping him."

Tanner went stiff while Faye became alert, but it was Caden's reaction that I saw the most. He'd gone impossibly still, his chest barely rising as his jaw became as hard as granite. The air above his head seemed to ripple, reminding me of how flames distorted the air. My breath caught as the faintest outline of a…of a crown began to appear on his head.

"Go on," he said, his voice deceptively level.

My heart thrummed as I stared at him. I'd only see the flaming, burnt crown and sword once before. Both seemed to have appeared out of thin air, and then disappeared again into it. The near presence was both fascinating and unsettling.

I swallowed. "He said that it was a member of the Summer Court who wished to see the return of Queen Morgana," I told them. "I think…I think he went to meet with this fae while he had me."

"Impossible," breathed Tanner. "No Summer fae would ever want such an atrocity as she to breach this world."

"Did he ever say how he planned to do so?" Caden asked.

I remembered, and I wasn't sure if telling him would cause that crown to make a complete appearance. "He said that it was unlikely for you to complete the prophecy, but he believed he could force you to open the gates. Is that possible? Can you open the gates without the prophecy?"

A muscle ticked in Caden's jaw. "I can."

That seemed to be news to both Tanner and Faye. "How?" she asked.

"If properly motivated, I could open a gateway," Caden said, the air settling above his head as his gaze held mine.

"You mean you could simply open one?" Faye asked. "Like turn a doorknob and…bam, it's open?"

My heart started pounding as flickers of memories surged. Aric had been searching for the King's *mortuus*, believing that he could use the person to force the King to open the gateway. It wasn't until he figured out that I'd been given the Summer Kiss that he realized I was the *mortuus*.

"Yes," Caden answered. "Obviously, that is information not widely known, and it needs to stay that way."

"Obviously," Tanner sputtered. "Especially with the Order. They would view you as a threat—"

"And that would be the last thing they ever viewed if so." Caden snarled, and a shiver of goosebumps spread across my flesh. His golden eyes burned. "It's not something I would do."

Unless.

That one word wasn't spoken, but I knew it hung in the silence between us.

And that was the moment I knew Caden's reaction had more to do with what Aric could've shared with this Summer fae. Aric could've told the fae traitor that I was the King's *mortuus*. His greatest weakness that could be used to control him.

"You can't stay here," Caden said. "You will stay with me."

My mouth dropped open in surprise. Partly because I hadn't thought he'd say something like that in front of Tanner and Faye, and also because he thought he could just state that and I'd go along with it.

"I'm not planning to stay here forever," I told him. "Luce said I just need to stay the rest of the week, and then I can go home."

"I don't want you to live here. I want you at my place where I can make sure you're safe. If you don't want to go to my place, I'll take you to yours. Luce will just have to deal with that."

A tumbling motion swept through my stomach. Caden and I staying together couldn't happen. I obviously didn't have the willpower necessary to keep from kissing him within five seconds of seeing him. There was no way I could do what I needed to do if he was living with me. No way at all.

Caden's eyes narrowed.

I squared my shoulders as I lifted my chin. "I don't recall asking you to stay with me or giving you permission."

"I don't recall needing either of those things."

"Are you serious?" I demanded, rising to my feet. "Of course, you need my permission to stay at my house."

He glared up at me. "Under normal circumstances, yes. But when it's to keep you out of harm's way, I don't."

"Yeah, that's not some unspoken law or something. And even if it were, I don't need to follow it. I'm not fae. You're not my King."

"Um," Faye murmured, shifting from one foot to the other uncomfortably.

"I know exactly what I am to you." Caden rose to his full height, but he didn't step toward me. I gaped at him. "This isn't up for discussion."

"That we can agree on, because you're not staying with me."

His smile was slow, predatory. "Then you're staying with me."

"No, I'm not!" I shouted. "I'm staying here until I can go home at the end of the week and sleep in my own bed—"

"I like where this is heading," he cut in.

Tanner made a choking sound.

I stepped forward. "By myself. I'm going home at the end of the week. By myself."

He quirked a brow. "We'll see."

Anger flashed through me hotly. "We won't see crap. You're not—"

"Okay. Let's all take a breather." Tanner had stood, holding up his hands. "No matter where Brighton decides to go at the end of the week, I am sure that she is not in any danger here. Aric is dead, and if what he said was true, which is unlikely, no Summer fae would seek to harm her, especially not here."

"I will rip the skin from any fae who even has the smallest inkling of looking at her in a way I do not like," Caden bit out.

My eyes widened. "That's a bit excessive."

Caden didn't take his gaze from me. "That's your opinion."

My hands curled into fists. "That's a mentally healthy opinion."

"You know damn well that it's not excessive," he all but growled.

"If you're worried about Brighton's safety, I'm sure that Ivy or even Faye would be willing to stay with her after she leaves. I will also make sure she's watched while here," Tanner tried again, and Faye nodded while I bristled at the idea of being under surveillance, even if necessary.

"I will make sure she is safe here," Caden replied.

Tanner appeared beyond flustered. "I mean this with all due respect, my King, I know that Brighton is important to you, but you must think about how this will look to Tatiana and her brother."

Caden's head snapped in his direction. "Do I appear as if I remotely care how it looks?"

The breath I took was as sharp as the one I knew Tanner inhaled. "You should care," I told him, and I had no idea how he didn't crack his neck with how fast he turned those furious eyes on me.

I had a feeling that whatever was about to come out of his mouth would be tantamount to me taking out an ad announcing that I was his *mortuus*.

Thank God that Faye spoke when she did. "Not to interrupt this very awkward conversation, but a Summer fae wanting the Queen to enter the human world? Do you really think one of our own would be working with Aric? With the Winter fae?"

"As if it hasn't happened before," Caden snapped. "Let's not forget that Aric was one of my closest confidants. He was my Knight. So, it's not just possible, it's extremely likely."

Chapter 5

I hadn't believed that Aric had lied, but knowing that Caden saw it as highly likely was like watching a pall of death settle over the normally warm hotel.

Tanner was in shock. I couldn't blame him. Faye looked as if she wanted to start a Fae Inquisition, and Caden looked like...

Well, I was doing my best not to see what he looked like by studiously ignoring him. Wasn't exactly doing much since I didn't need to see him to know that he was mad. His fury was in every clipped response and the tension that bled from him. I didn't know what he was angrier about—that someone in his own Court had betrayed him, or that I had pushed back on the idea of him staying with me.

There was no way I could allow that to happen.

I kept trying to leave while Tanner and Faye discussed who the traitor could be. Still, every time I moved an inch, either Faye would ask if there was anything else I could remember, or Caden sent me a look that froze me in my tracks.

Which caused my irritation to skyrocket to uncharted territories. I would've loved for Caden to stay with me. For him to be there with me. But that was beside the point. Even if things were hunky-dory between us, I wouldn't be cool with his high-handed attitude. I had a say in this. The final say. And he needed to get that through his thick, albeit sexy, skull.

Finally, after it was agreed that Kalen, another fae, and Ren and Ivy would be advised about the potential traitor in our midst, Tanner and Faye headed for the door. It had also been decided that it would be best to keep the knowledge of Caden's ability to open the gateway limited to those in the room. As Tanner had said, there was no need to cause undue distrust and weaken the fledgling bond between the Summer fae and the Order...if one could call the sliver of a thread brought about by an agreement to work together a bond.

I rose, my gaze fixed on the door as if it were a lifeline. It was far past time to act like the entire future of the human and fae race, of our child, depended on us—or me—making the right choice. *Our child*. Those words caused my heart to start pounding. I made it about two steps.

"Brighton."

A tiny, childish part of me wanted to pretend as if I hadn't heard him. I was a lot of things, but a coward wasn't one of them. I stopped.

Okay. Maybe I was a little bit cowardly, because I didn't face him. I could feel him though. He couldn't be standing more than a few feet behind me.

"Talk to me."

"About what?"

"Don't pretend that you don't know." He was closer now. I could practically feel his heat against my back, and it took everything in me not to turn around and throw my arms around him. To revel in that warmth and comfort once more.

I stayed where I was. "Maybe I just don't want to talk about what I know you want to discuss."

"And maybe I don't want to stand here and talk to the back of your head, but that's what I'm doing."

"You stopped me," I pointed out.

There was a beat of silence. "What is going on, Brighton?"

Sighing, I faced him because he didn't deserve to talk to my haphazard ponytail. Even though I'd been sitting in the same room with him, had been in his lap and had been kissing him just a bit ago, I still felt a little breathless when I met his gaze. There was such openness in his striking features, not at all like when I'd first gotten to know him.

"Why are you so resistant to coming home with me or staying with you?" he asked. "You know damn well it's necessary. If Aric told anyone that you're my *mortuus*, you're in danger."

My chest hollowed. I didn't want to be in danger. Not after what I'd gone through, but it wasn't like my life hadn't been risky before. As a member of the Order, even one that wasn't expected to patrol like the other members, I still had a target on my back, as history had proven. "We really don't know if Aric told this Summer fae traitor anything. It wasn't like he lived long after realizing what I was."

"But it's also not like you killed him the moment after he realized what you meant to me, right?" he challenged.

I hadn't. "All that means is that we don't know."

"And that is why we need to be extra cautious. I will not allow harm to come to you. Not again." His chin dipped as those fiery eyes met mine. "Never again."

His words brought forth too much pleasure. "I can protect myself, Caden."

"Didn't say you couldn't, but why should you have to do that by yourself?"

I folded my arms over my chest, mainly to stop myself from looping them around his neck. "Because I always have."

He took a small, measured step forward. "But things are different. You have me now. You have all of me."

It felt like a knife being shoved straight into my heart. His words shouldn't make me feel that way. They should bring me nothing but happiness.

This isn't fair.

It really wasn't, but that didn't change reality. "I don't want you to protect me," I forced out, each word stinging and scraping at me. "I don't want you at my house. I don't—I don't want you."

His brows lifted. That was the only response he showed.

I drew in a shallow, burning breath. "Thank you for everything you've done for me, but I can't... I can't do this with you. I care about you, but I...I don't want to be with you."

"You don't?" His tone was flat.

Another sharp, piercing stab to the chest as I said, "I don't love you."

"Is that so?"

I blinked at the response, unsure how to proceed. I didn't know how he'd react. Maybe argue? Get mad? Sad? The deadpanned replies threw me off. Would it be this easy? If so, did he even really love me?

It doesn't matter.

It did, though.

Confused and irritated with myself, I took a step back. "I'm sorry."

His head tilted slightly. "For what?"

"Everything," I whispered.

Caden's jaw tightened. "Are you done now?"

"Done what?"

"Done lying?"

I jolted. "I'm not lying."

"Bullshit," he said, and I tensed. "I don't know what's going on, but I know there's something. You're not telling me something."

Ice drenched my skin. "I'm telling you how I really feel—"

"And I'm telling you that you don't even believe the words coming out of your mouth. Neither do I. What you're saying is not what you want."

"It—"

"It's not the truth," he continued, the fire in his eyes flaming. "I *know* it's not."

I snapped my mouth shut as the walls around me seemed to press in. Was it possible that what he sensed of my emotions could betray me that much? I wasn't sure, especially since I could barely make sense of everything that I was feeling.

Turning into the coward I didn't think I was, I said, "I can't do this right now. I'm really tired and just want to go lay down."

Caden appeared as if he wished to continue, but after a moment, he said, "This conversation isn't over, Brighton."

How I wished that it wasn't. "But it is," I whispered, and then I walked out of the room, my heart in tatters.

* * * *

I'd gone straight to my room and climbed into bed, curling onto my side and squeezing my eyes shut against the flood of tears that threatened to burst free.

I hurt. My heart hurt. And I couldn't think about what I'd just done and how incredibly wrong it'd felt. I forced myself to sleep, thinking that would be better than lying awake and feeling what I did now. So I slept the day and night away. I woke in the morning to find a covered plate of scrambled eggs and toast sitting in the chair Caden had occupied. I'd devoured the food by the time Luce showed to check on me. She was pleased and a bit surprised by how quickly my injuries were healing. I'd asked about the food, thinking she'd had it sent up, but she hadn't. I tried not to think of who had while I asked if it was possible for Luce to pick me up some prenatal vitamins. Already ahead of me, she pulled a small bottle from the pocket of her white lab coat. According to Luce, a pregnant fae didn't need the extra vitamins, but considering that I was human, and given the lack of nutrition I'd experienced in the early weeks of pregnancy, she believed it would be wise for me to take them.

I hid them in the dresser drawer.

After, I'd slept for most of the day, waking once when Ivy came to visit and then again in the late afternoon. The first thing I looked at when I opened my eyes was the chair.

Caden wasn't sitting there, but another covered dish was.

Sitting up far more easily than I had the day before, I lifted the lid and found a warm bowl of soup that smelled of rich, flavorful herbs. There were two slices of thick, toasted bread beside it. My stomach grumbled.

Did Ivy bring this up?

Had it been Caden?

I stared at the food for what felt like a small eternity, just like I had that morning. A sense of unease mingled with the hunger, leaving me vaguely nauseous. Trepidation was acid in my veins. A fine tremor coursed through my arm as I reached for the food. I didn't realize what I was doing until I caught myself looking around the room, making sure…

Making sure it was empty.

No one was here. No one was going to hurt me. Aric was dead. I was safe.

I still hesitated.

God, I hated this—hated that I associated food with pain now. Eating was…well, it was a favorite pastime of mine. I *loved* to eat.

Cursing under my breath, I snatched up the plate. Creamy soup sloshed over the side of the bowl. I grabbed the spoon and started hauling the liquid into my mouth, not even slowing down to really enjoy it. I shoveled bread in next, chewing enough that I didn't choke. Every time thoughts of Caden, Aric, of *anything* began to creep in, I shoved them aside. By the time the bowl was empty and only crumbs remained on the plate, the unease had faded to a shadow.

I placed my hand on my stomach. I needed to get over this whole food thing. I was eating for two now.

That thought caused a half-hysterical-sounding giggle and a stunning realization. I wanted a family. A husband. A child. It wasn't something I'd ever really consciously acknowledged, and it wasn't as if I believed one needed a significant other or offspring to make a family, but that was what *I* desired. I wanted to give a child what I didn't have—a father who was alive and not just present or active in a child's life, but also *there*. I wanted to be the mother that mine couldn't be—at no fault of her own. The realization brought forth a wave of aching yearning for what I wanted so badly but could not have.

I waited until I was sure my stomach wasn't going to revolt and then I rose, leaving the room. I already knew I couldn't just sit in here like I'd done. If I did, my brain would start going down roads best not traveled. I needed to move around—do something. The faint glow of sunlight still crept under the blinds. Moving to the dresser, I rooted around until I found a cardigan. I slipped it on and then made my way to the first floor. I kept my eyes downcast as I passed fae going in and out of the cafeteria and the common areas. Reaching the glass doors, I looked up as they parted. Cool, early evening air washed over me as I stepped out into a courtyard that was so beautiful it often seemed unreal to me.

I secretly believed that this had to be how the Otherworld looked, at least at some point in time. Tall trees rose up in the deep blue sky. Vines climbed trellises, and a variety of flowers bloomed, unaffected by the chillier temperatures as they scented the air with sweet and musky undertones. Paper lanterns hung from the branches, always lit. String lights crisscrossed over the stone pathway and led to little sitting areas hidden away.

This was a favorite place of mine, and whenever I visited Hotel Good Fae and got the chance to explore the courtyard, I did.

Reaching out, I skimmed my fingers over the slick vines. No matter what I did with my own courtyard, I could never hope for it to look like this. Not even when Mom was still alive. Gardening had seemed to ground her, keeping her in this world. If Caden weren't correct about my mind being stronger due to the Summer Kiss, maybe I could seek refuge in the garden as well.

God, I hoped he was right. Glancing up at the sky, I prayed that he was. The child I carried in me needed a mother—

"Lite Bright?"

That voice. That name. Heart leaping into my throat, I spun around. "*Tink*."

Chapter 6

Standing several feet back on the pathway, the brownie was in his full-sized form. He was well over six feet tall, and even in the fading sunlight, I saw that he looked different. I'd have to be missing my eyeballs not to notice it.

His normally shockingly white hair was a dark brown.

"Your hair!"

He stood there, arms at his sides, and I knew with his vision, he could clearly see my face. "Who cares about my hair right now," he said, and then he moved.

Tink crossed the distance between us, and in a nanosecond, he swept me up. My feet left the ground as the right side of my cheek was planted to his chest. My ribs and the numerous bruises protested the embrace, but I didn't say a word as I hugged him back just as tightly.

I'd missed him so much.

Sure, he could be a handful sometimes—okay, most of the time. His short stay with me had turned into more of a permanent roommate situation, unbeknownst to me. I was constantly tripping over the numerous boxes shipped from Amazon, he almost always left some sort of mess behind, and on more than one occasion, he'd given me a minor heart attack by hiding while in brownie-sized form under the covers or in cabinets. But I'd missed him.

Slowly, he lowered me to my feet and pulled back, keeping his arms around me. His gaze searched my face in the waning light. "I didn't know."

"Tink—"

"I was lounging on the beach, drinking super fruity cocktails, getting my suntan on, and enjoying being treated like the last brownie in this world and any other. And I had no idea." His eyes glistened. "I had no idea this was being done to you."

My chest ached. "It's okay."

"No, it's not," he replied softly. "Each time I called and either Ivy or Ren or the King answered, my super-brownie senses told me something was up. But they assured me you were fine, and that the Order had you working on a special project or some shit. I should've known better. The Order hardly uses you for anything."

"Well, that's not necessarily true…"

"But Fabian told me I shouldn't worry, and he suggested that we stay longer," he continued as if I hadn't spoken. "I believed him. I wanted to believe him, even though I knew something was wrong. I was living my best life, and you were fighting for yours."

"That's not your fault." I gripped the front of his shirt. "They didn't want you to worry when there was nothing to be done."

"I get that. I do. That's the only reason I haven't killed any of them, including Fabian. And trust me," he said, voice hardening, "I am more than capable of killing each and every one of them."

I blinked. Sometimes it was easy to forget that Tink wasn't just an amusing Otherworlder able to change sizes. He was one of the most powerful Otherworld beings alive, who happened to have an addiction to Amazon Prime, *Harry Potter*, and *Twilight*.

"I could've done something. I could've looked for you. I could've found—"

"No one was able to find me. Not even the King until…until he did," I said, tugging on Tink's shirt. "You would've just been worrying and—"

"And that's what I should've been doing. You're my Lite Bright. I'm your Tink. I should've known. And I may or may not punch Ivy when I see her."

"Don't punch Ivy."

"Not even a little?"

"No."

"How about a love tap?"

A sob settled in the back of my throat as I shook my head no.

"What about when I'm tiny Tink-sized with teeny, tiny fists?"

I choked on a laugh. "Ren would still skewer you with a toothpick."

"I'd punch him first. He's had it coming since I had to unexpectedly see his junk in Ivy's kitchen."

Another laugh left me. "I've missed you," I said, face-planting against his chest.

"Of course, you did. I'm awesome." He cleared his throat. There was a pause, and I felt his lips brush the top of my head. "Fabian told me what really happened when we were about an hour out from here. I almost caused a massive pileup on the interstate."

My lips twitched.

His hands settled on my shoulders and he guided me back. "He said you killed him. Aric?"

"I did," I whispered.

"Is there anything left of his body?"

"Um, no. He sort of just disintegrated, like most Ancients."

"Not even ashes?"

"I don't think so."

"I'll ask the King."

I frowned. "Why?"

"Because I want to take a shit on his remains."

"Oh my God." I laughed again. "That is so disgusting."

"I know. It's the most disrespectful thing I can think of," he explained and then led me toward a loveseat that often reminded me of a birdcage sliced open. "Tell me, Bri. Tell me everything you can."

As we sat on the thick cushions, and the gauzy curtain draped over the chair rippled in the breeze, I told him everything I could remember. It wasn't the first time, but there was a sense that the weight was lifting, just a little this time around. It was like letting out a breath.

"The King is most likely right," Tink said after I told him about the hallucination I'd had earlier. "Your mind is stronger."

"I hope so."

"It could have nothing to do with the feedings." He was toying with my hair. Somehow, it had come out of its ponytail. "It could be that post-traumatic syndrome thing that sometimes causes people to hoard things in their houses."

I arched a brow. "You watch way too much television."

"But I could be right. You experienced some trauma. Hearing voices, reliving the events is pretty common afterwards, according to Dr. Phil."

I stared at him.

"After I saw Ren's junk, I kept seeing it. Sometimes, it would talk to me—"

"You're a mess."

He grinned at me. "Fabian told me something else."

"What?"

"He told me how the King nearly tore the city apart looking for you," he said, and every muscle in my body tensed. "Wouldn't give up on finding you. He also said that Ivy told him he's barely left your side since he found you."

I looked away. "You know that I helped him when he was wounded. He felt like he owed me—"

"Are you forgetting that I saw him kiss you like you were a snack?"

My cheeks heated. "No, I'm not forgetting that, but you know he's the King and I'm…it doesn't matter. Tell me about your hair. Please?"

Momentarily distracted, he ran his hand through his locks. It wasn't spiky but fell over his forehead. "Do you like it?"

"I …I do." The color matched his brows now, and somehow made him appear more adult. Which was weird, but the darker color suited him. In all honesty, any color fit him. Tink was gorgeous. "It's just a shock."

"I didn't recognize myself when I saw my reflection. It was strange." He lifted a shoulder. "I sort of got bored with it, you know? Fabian suggested I should color it, and since I was bored, I thought YOLO, bitches. Fabian did it for me." His voice lowered. "He didn't wear gloves. It took days for the dye to fade from his hands."

"Oh no." I grinned. "But he did a good job."

"He does a good job at everything. It's annoying, and I mean that in the best way." The smile on his face faded. "Lite Bright…"

"I'm okay. I really am. I know I don't look it, but I'm fine." I changed the subject once more. "Where's Dixon?"

"Fabian has him. Carrying him around in the sling."

I sort of wished I could see that.

"I know he loves you."

"What?" I squeaked, my gaze shooting back to his.

"He spoke to Fabian before we got here. I don't know exactly what he said, but Fabian knows his brother." Tink lightly touched my arm. "He also told Fabian what he did."

There could be several things that Caden might've told him.

"He ended his engagement."

I closed my eyes. Why did it have to be that?

"I honestly thought that when I got here, I'd find you with him. So, color me surprised when he told us you were out in the courtyard by yourself."

My eyes opened as my lips pursed. I couldn't say that I was shocked that Caden knew exactly where I was.

"And here you are, acting like nothing's going on when the motherfucking King of the Summer Court is in love with you." He tapped my arm again. "I know you like him. You like him a lot, and you were hurt when he pushed you away."

"Things have...they've changed. I've been through a lot," I said, hating that I was using what'd happened to me as an excuse.

"Bri, you've been through a lot. But, girl, you'd already been through a lot. You're a fighter. You're a survivor," he said, and my gaze lifted to his. "What you've gone through is terrible. But I don't think it sucked out your ability to love and the ability to recognize the feeling. Or your common sense."

"My common sense?"

"Yes. Your common sense seems to have taken a vacation," he said, and my brows lifted. "You have the love and devotion of a King. Granted, he's not human, but who in their right mind would swipe left on him?"

"That's the problem, Tink. He's the King."

"So? That should fall under the pro category," he reasoned.

I stared at him. "Do you know what will happen if he doesn't choose a Queen from his people? I know you do. That's why you got all quiet and weird after you saw him kiss me. That's why you tried to get me to understand that he had reasons for pushing me away."

"You're right, but he still chose you. He chose you over his Court, over—"

"And you know what that means." I couldn't hear how he chose me. That wasn't helping. "You know what will happen."

"Is that why you're saying things are different now?"

"Why else would I say it?" I admitted, shoulders slumping.

His gaze roamed over me, and his chest rose with a heavy breath. "You love him, right?"

"That doesn't matter."

"It's the only thing that matters," he responded. "Despite what and who he is, you still fell in love with him. Is that not true?"

I wanted to be able to say no, and maybe that would be the right thing to do. I needed to get better at saying it because perhaps then I'd believe it. But I couldn't lie to Tink. "Yes," I whispered. "But you can't tell him that."

He arched a brow. "You think he doesn't already know?"

"It doesn't matter what he knows or thinks. He needs a Queen, and the last thing he or I need is for someone to confirm how I feel."

"You mean confirm what he already knows." Tink looked out over the darkened courtyard while I debated punching him, but since I'd just told him he couldn't punch Ivy, I couldn't turn around and do it to him. "I know what could happen. Sure, the Court would weaken, and they'd be without a King, but that doesn't mean fae will start dropping dead everywhere." He sat back against the thick, cream-colored cushion. "It doesn't mean that the King will become so weakened that he can't defend himself. It doesn't mean that you should both sacrifice what you deserve. Love is more important."

"You really believe that? That Caden and I being together is more important than the survival of the fae? Of the human race and our—?" I cut myself off as my stomach dropped.

His eyes shot to mine. "And what?"

"Nothing."

"Liar. What were you going to say?"

Shaking my head, I looked away. "It's nothing, Tink."

He was quiet for a moment. "What are you not telling me?"

"Why does everyone keep asking me that?" I threw up my hands in frustration. Okay. Only he and Caden had said that, but whatever.

"Maybe because there's obviously something you're not sharing." There was a pause. "I'm offended."

"Are you now?"

"Yes. I'm Tink. We're roomies. We have joint custody of Dixon."

My brows puckered. "We do not have joint custody of your cat."

"Not true. He sleeps in your bed. That means we have joint custody whether you're aware of it or not," he said. "And you're keeping something from me. You're not telling me the truth, and I've just spent weeks with everyone keeping the truth from me. I expected better from you."

My mouth dropped open as I stared at him. A trickle of guilt crept into me, which I was sure he'd intended. "That is so manipulative."

"Is it working?"

A short laugh escaped me as my gaze traveled to where my arms were folded over my stomach. I opened my mouth and then closed it. The need to confide in Tink—in anyone—hit me hard. It hadn't even been a day, and I was bursting to tell someone.

And Tink…if he was still living with me in a few months, would know. It would eventually become noticeable. I couldn't hide it from everyone. I needed someone who knew. I could confide in Ivy, but she was prone to outbursts, and there was her own messy history with Caden.

Lifting my hands, I scrubbed them down my face, covering my mouth. "If I tell you this, you have to promise me you won't say anything."

"I promise," he agreed quickly.

"I mean it, Tink. You're going to want to say something, but you can't repeat this. Not to Fabian or Ivy or even Dixon."

"What in the hell would Dixon do? He's a cat."

"I don't care." Lowering my hands, I looked at him. "You can't repeat this. If you do, I will…" I searched for the worst possible thing that could happen to Tink. "I will find a way to blacklist you from Amazon, and until then, I will throw every single one of your packages in the garbage. I will cancel your orders. I'll discontinue the internet."

His eyes widened as he pressed his hand to his chest. "That's harsh."

"I know." I held his gaze. "Do you still want to know?"

Tink tilted his head. "I can keep a secret, Bri. You have no idea how many secrets I already keep. I'm practically the keeper of secrets. You all don't even know my real name."

I frowned. "What is your real name?"

He smirked.

"Does Fabian know?"

"Nope."

"For real?"

"For reals."

I was kind of surprised that he hadn't told Fabian. There was power in knowing a fae's true name. I nibbled on my lip and then it sort of just spilled out of me. Two simple words that were incredibly life-altering. "I'm pregnant."

Tink blinked slowly. "With a baby?"

"What other thing would I be pregnant with?" I asked.

He gave a little shake of his head, and then a wide, beautiful smile broke out across his face, briefly stunning me. "Does that mean I get to be a godfather? I've always wanted to be a godfather. I can babysit. There are so many things I can show this child. I can make his or her toys come to life. Did you know that? I can teach them the wonders of *Harry Potter* and *Twilight*. Oh! And *Game of Thrones*. Well, that will probably have to come later. But think of all—" He came to a grinding halt while I gaped at him.

Tink drew back from me and then stood, lifting his hands. "I'm about to ask a potentially obvious question here. Bear with me while I collect myself."

"Yes, it's Caden's child," I stated dryly.

"You didn't bear with me!"

"Tink."

He clasped his hands together under his chin. "You are having his child?"

I nodded.

"You are carrying a baby inside you right now that has your and his DNA?"

"Yes."

Tink bent at the waist so we were at eye level with each other. "You are impregnated by him?"

"Yes. Yes, Tink. I'm pregnant. He's the father. Caden's the dad," I told him, exasperated. "The King is the father."

"Holy shit."

I snapped my mouth shut.

Tink blinked.

My heart stopped as my belly rolled all the way to the tips of my toes. Neither of us had said that.

Tink straightened.

I looked over his shoulder.

And I saw not one, not two, but *three* fae staring at us in utter shock.

Chapter 7

It was the fair-haired Kalen who'd spoken. He looked as shocked as I felt. Standing beside him, Faye looked as if a slight breeze might knock her flat on her back. And of all people to be here, Tanner was with them.

He looked like he was seconds away from vomiting.

The five of us just stared at one another in silence while my heart pounded against my ribs. I thought I might hurl. Tanner and I could go puke together.

Tink was the first to break the silence.

"I dyed my hair," Tink announced. "Do you all like it? I think it complements my skin tone."

For the first time in, well, forever, Tanner ignored Tink. "You're pregnant," the leader of the hotel said. "By…" He seemed as if he couldn't bring himself to say it.

My throat dried. "I…"

"We heard her," Faye said, blinking as her features settled into their typical blandness. "I don't think we need her to repeat it."

This couldn't possibly be any worse.

Well, if Caden had been with them, that would have been worse.

"I knew…" Tanner paused for a rough inhale. "I knew there was something between the two of you. It was obvious even before your abduction. I thought it was a passing fancy, but the way he behaved while you were missing told me it was more."

"Told everyone it was more," Kalen muttered under his breath.

"Now I understand his reaction earlier, why he demanded to be with you—"

"Wait." I shot out of the chair. "He doesn't know."

"What?" Faye's brows lifted.

"I haven't told him. I don't plan to tell him—"

"What?" Tink echoed in a demanding tone.

Kalen pinched the bridge of his nose. "I have a feeling I'm going to regret coming out here tonight."

"What do you mean you're not planning to tell him?" Tanner asked.

"In other words, are you out of your freaking mind?" Tink cried.

"This is like one of those daytime talk shows," commented Faye.

Kalen glanced at her. "You're thinking of *Maury*?"

The female fae nodded.

"Love that show," Tink chimed in.

"He behaved that way and doesn't know you're carrying his youngling?" Tanner asked.

"I'm going to be the godfather," Tink announced.

"Thoughts and prayers for that child," Kalen said.

"I know humans have their own views on these types of matters." Tanner lifted his chin. "But we believe that the father has the same rights as a mother—"

"Okay, everyone needs to shut up for a second, stop judging me and listen," I snapped, a fine sheen of sweat dotting my brow. "I just found out today, and I am planning to tell him eventually. But not right now. None of you are going to say a word to him. For two reasons. Number one—it's none of your business."

Tanner sucked in air, looking absolutely affronted. "He is our King."

"And this is still not your business," I told him. "The second reason is because I'm trying to do the right thing, and that does not involve giving him a congratulations card at the moment."

Kalen's brow wrinkled.

"I'm about to tell you all something that I hope shines a whole new light on this situation. Caden chose me. Not his betrothed. Not any other fae. He ended his engagement with Tatiana." The stunned gasps from the three fae echoed like thunder. "I don't think he's going to pick another fae, and I'm sure as hell not into a party of three. He loves me. I love him, but I know what will happen if he doesn't choose a Queen. I know what's at stake. I assume each of you understands as well."

Tanner was slow to nod, even though he looked a little green under his silvery skin.

"So I know that no matter what I want, what he wants, it can't be." My voice warbled, and when Tink opened his mouth, I pointed my finger at him. "I do not need to hear how love is worth everything. Do you think I don't want to run in there and throw my arms around him and never let go? This isn't easy for me, but I am pregnant. I am going to have a child. And even though I have no idea how to even raise a kid, I know I don't want to bring him or her into a world that will go to hell in a handbasket. I know Caden needs to marry one of his own. I know the entire fae race and all humans depend on that. So, no. I'm not telling him anything until he's happily married. Then, I will tell him."

Breathing heavily, I willed the knot of emotion swelling in my chest to fade. It had to. "So if any of you have any hope of preventing a catastrophe from happening, then you will keep your mouths shut about this, and you will do everything in your power to make—" I tried to swallow, but the knot had crept into my throat. "Everything in your power to make sure he marries Tatiana or another fae. That's what you should be doing. But if you tell him what you overheard... I don't know what he'll do." Pressing my lips together, I shook my head as I remembered him talking about his sister Scorcha. I tried to push away the image of him brushing the knots out of a little girl's hair. I tried to forget how careful and gentle he was when he did it for me. I cleared my throat. "I have no idea what he'd do, but it won't help to make sure the right thing is done. That much I do know."

No one spoke.

Not even Tink. Not for a long time.

It was Tanner who finally did.

"You are doing the right thing," he said. At his sides, his hands were opening and closing.

Finally! Finally, someone realized that I was doing the right thing. There was no relief, though. No joy. Just a heaviness that threatened to drag me to the ground and then through it.

"It gives me no pleasure to hide anything from my King, nor does knowing what you must be going through. But the future of our Court and of this world is paramount and trumps our needs and desires," he continued. I felt myself nodding slowly. "We'll keep your confidence, Brighton."

Sitting down in the chair, all the energy went right out of me. "Thank you."

His mouth tightened.

"Neither Faye nor Kalen will repeat a word of what was overheard or discussed here," Tanner announced, and for the first time, I saw his mask of civility slip a little, revealing the deadly creature underneath as he looked to the two of them. "Do you understand me?"

Faye looked uncomfortable but she nodded. "I do."

"I was right. I regret this." Beside her, Kalen thrust a hand through his hair. "I don't like this. He's our King."

"I'm not asking if you like it." Authority bled into Tanner's tone. "None of us do. But we must do things we don't like to protect the future, no matter how distasteful we find them." His hands stilled as his gaze met mine. "And I promise you that what you're doing will not be in vain. I will do everything in my power to ensure that."

I nodded again because I felt distasteful. I felt wrung out. I felt everything and nothing as Tanner bid us goodbye. The others followed, but Kalen stopped and whispered something in Tink's ear. The brownie nodded solemnly. At any other time, I would've been curious to know what was said, but right then, I didn't have the brain capacity for it.

Tink sat beside me. "So…"

Wearily, I looked over at him.

"That was awkward."

I laughed, but it didn't feel right. "Do you think they'll keep silent?"

"I believe so."

"And you?" I whispered.

"Of course. I don't want you to throw away my packages."

I smiled at that.

He leaned in, resting his forehead against mine. "You know what I think?"

I was half afraid to ask. "What?"

"I think you'll make a good mom. After all, I'm one hell of a test run."

* * * *

I spent the following two days with Fabian and Tink as my shadows. If I wanted to go out into the courtyard, they went with me. If I stayed in my room, they kept me company by either joining me on the bed to watch bad reality television or a movie in the living room area of the suite. I didn't think I'd ever spent that much time in bed with one man before, let alone two. I knew they were there because Caden wasn't, and I had a feeling they were with me at his request. Not that I believed they didn't want to spend time with me, but it wasn't like I was great to be around. I was the living embodiment of morose.

I hadn't talked to Caden since I'd told him I didn't love him, but I woke in the middle of the night, swearing that his scent was in the room. Often, when I was in the courtyard with Fabian and Tink, a shivery wave of awareness broke out along the back of my neck and over my skin. I'd turn, fully expecting to find Caden there, looking at me in that intense way of his. But he was never there, just like when I woke in the night—the room was empty.

I couldn't make sense of how I felt. I didn't know what to think or feel. A stupid part of me had been pleased to know that Caden had possibly been the one to deliver the food or could be watching me while I was in the courtyard. The other half of me wanted to punch myself in the face.

Tanner and the others had kept their vow so far. I figured I would know if they'd told Caden about the pregnancy, but when I walked out to the courtyard with Fabian and Tink Friday evening, I saw that he was diligently working to make sure that Caden chose a Queen.

Stepping out into the courtyard, I felt as if I'd been sucker punched in the heart when I saw Caden standing to the right, under several softly glowing paper lanterns. Wearing black trousers and a white button-down shirt, with his hair loose and brushing broad shoulders, he looked as if he'd stepped off the cover of a magazine or out of some fantasy. He wasn't alone. Tanner was with him, as were several other fae, including Kalen. So was the tall and elegant, raven-haired Tatiana. Her brother, who was equally striking with his dark hair and deep, silvery hued skin, was also there.

There was a slight smile playing across Caden's face as Tatiana said something to him. She reached across the scant distance between them and touched the forearm exposed by the rolled-up sleeve of his shirt.

There was no mistaking that Caden and Tatiana would make a stunning couple found only in fairy tales and seeing them together made me painfully aware of the fact that no one in their right mind would ever believe that he'd chosen me over someone so flawless. So graceful.

The bite of jealousy took a huge chunk out of my heart even as I told myself I should be relieved. I should be happy to see him speaking with her. It wasn't like him finding another fae to marry would lessen the blow if he rekindled the arrangement with Tatiana.

Tink had taken my hand the moment we spotted them and began talking about sea turtles. Or possibly opossums. I wasn't sure. Caden appeared wholly unaware of us. The only person who seemed to know we were there was Sterling, Tatiana's brother. His gaze tracked us until I could no longer tell if he was watching.

The courtyard had lost some of its beauty that night, and I hadn't lingered long. Caden and the group of fae were gone when we went back inside, but based on the amount of activity behind the frosted glass of the common room, I had a feeling the King was in there. There was a lot of laughter, and I thought I even detected music. I'd heard that they often threw parties, sometimes for birthdays or weddings, and other times just because. Envy joined jealousy, and the moment I was in my hotel room, I managed to get Fabian and Tink to leave. I hoped they joined whatever was going on downstairs. They belonged there. I didn't. And while I knew I wouldn't be unwelcome—well, I doubted Tanner would be thrilled if I made my presence known since he was obviously working hard to reconnect Caden and Tatiana. But I also knew that I was an outsider, no matter my relationship with Tink or Prince Fabian.

Feeling older and wearier than I had in a very long time, I pulled on a sleep shirt that Ivy had retrieved from my house. It was lightweight and long, reaching my thighs. I climbed into bed, shamefully early for a Friday night, beyond thankful that tonight was my last night here.

"I got this," I reminded myself as I had every night since Monday. As I placed my hand against my belly, I repeated, "We got this."

Drifting off, I wondered why it was so easy to fall asleep now when I'd always struggled to do so before. Was it the pregnancy? I'd read once that it could make you more tired. Or was it my body healing and recovering? The bruises and the cuts had all faded. My eyes were no longer swollen, and most of the slices had become only faint pink marks. Or was it depression? It was probably all of it.

The darkness of a dreamless sleep slowly broke apart, revealing damp bricks covered by thick, ropey vines. Two torches struggled to beat back the shadows of the…tomb.

My eyes widened as my heart stuttered. Under me, the stone was like a sheet of ice. I jackknifed up, but pressure around my neck choked me. Gasping, I pressed my fingers to my throat. Cool, hard metal.

No. No. No.

I wasn't there. I wasn't in the tomb. This had to be a nightmare. Shaking, I looked down at myself, recognizing the faded image of a mound of beignets on my sleep shirt. My gaze shot to where the door to the tomb was located and saw nothing but a void of nothingness. The abyss rippled out. Thick tendrils licked over the walls and drenched the floor, rapidly swallowing the tomb and me.

Wake up. Wake up. I need to—

"Miss me?"

The sound of Aric's voice in my ear sent a bolt of fear straight through me, and a scream tore from deep within me. I twisted, hands pushing out—

My palms connected with something hard and warm. Aric was never warm. His skin was always cold, his touch painfully frigid.

"It's me. Brighton, you're okay." A deep voice scattered the darkness. "You're safe."

Caden.

I opened my eyes, wincing. A bedside lamp had been turned on, casting the room in light that was normally soft. My pounding heartbeat accelerated as I realized that the hard, warm surface under my palms was the white button-down shirt covering Caden's chest.

Scrambling back to the center of the bed, my gaze flew to Caden's face. He was right there, perched on the edge of my mattress, several strands of hair falling forward to rest against his cheek.

He didn't blink as he stared back at me. "Brighton?"

"Yes?" I whispered, disorientated.

His gaze searched mine. "Are you all right?"

"I…I think I was having a nightmare."

"You were. You screamed."

"You heard me scream?"

He nodded.

Some of the fog lifted. "How did you hear me scream?"

"I was outside your room."

I started to ask what he had been doing there, but then it struck me. "You've been keeping watch during the night?"

Caden said nothing as he tucked the strands of hair back from his face.

My heart started pounding for a wholly different reason. "Have you've been doing that every night since…?"

"Since you lied straight to my face and walked out of the room?" he finished for me. "Yes, I have."

I jolted. "I didn't lie."

One eyebrow rose as thick lashes lifted.

I decided to ignore that look. "Why are you doing that? You're the

King. I am sure there are several fae you'd trust to keep watch."

"There is no one I trust enough to keep watch—"

"Besides your brother and Tink?" I interrupted.

"I trust them to a certain degree."

I thought about the sensation of awareness when I was in the courtyard as if he were there. The warring mix of emotion rose again.

"And if you have to ask why I'm the one watching over you, then I don't think I've been clear enough with you," he added.

Oh, he'd been clear, and I was desperately trying not to see the reasons. Maybe that was why the tiny piece of bitterness slipped out of me. "I'm surprised you're not busy right now with—" I managed to stop myself from finishing the sentence.

"With whom?" One side of his lips curved up. "Tatiana?"

I looked away.

"I saw you in the courtyard, Brighton. I wasn't there with Tatiana, but it seems where I go this week, Tanner finds me with Tatiana in tow."

I kept my face impressively blank. "I shouldn't have said anything. I don't even know why I did. And you shouldn't be here."

"I know what I should and should not do. Keeping you safe is something that I should be doing." His gaze lowered. "Checking out your legs at the moment would probably be one of the things I shouldn't be doing."

My legs?

I glanced down to discover that the blanket had slipped to my knees, and a whole lot of leg was visible. Flushing, I yanked the cover up. "I see knowing you shouldn't be doing something hasn't stopped you."

"You know you shouldn't lie to me, but yet you still do," he replied. "Why should you be the only one who does things they know they shouldn't?"

My grip tightened on the blanket. "For the last time, I—"

"Did I ever tell you that my mother always knew when I was lying?" he interrupted, throwing me off.

I shook my head. "No."

"She always claimed that I would look down and smile whenever I told an untruth. I didn't believe her. Who would smile when they lied?"

"Good question," I murmured.

"But then I started to pay attention, and she was right. Every time I lied, I looked down and felt my lips curving upward. It wasn't a large smile, but she was right." He grinned then as he drew a finger over the sheet, idly tracing a shape. "Of course, since I learned that she was right, I've managed to stop doing it. But she could never tell when Fabian lied. Used to irritate the hell out of me."

Unable to pretend that I was disinterested, I said, "Fabian has never struck me as the type who lies a lot."

He snorted. "Fabian lied about finishing his studying or where he was when he was supposed to be training or whatever. He lied as much as I did, but it was never anything harmful."

"Were any of your lies harmful?"

"Only one." His gaze lifted to mine. "But that was a long time after I learned to conceal a lie, and it wasn't all that long ago."

I thought about when he told me that what had happened between us hadn't been real. My stomach churned as all those terrible, sticky feelings came surging back. And now I was doing the same to him.

"My mother would be so incredibly disappointed to learn how good at lying I've become," he commented.

I dared a quick peek at him. "What happened to your mother? And father?"

"They died during the war with the Winter Court," he answered, his voice tinged with sorrow.

"I'm sorry."

"Thank you, but they died fighting for their people. I know both took great honor in that, and I take solace." He trailed off, shaking his head.

"What?"

"I shouldn't even admit this. It shows how incredibly selfish I can be, but I...I take solace in the fact that neither my father nor my mother was alive to see what became of me."

Sympathy squeezed my heart. "What became of you wasn't your fault. You were under the Queen's curse. I don't think your parents would hold what you did while under her control against you."

"They wouldn't have." His eyes met mine. "And that makes it all harder to comprehend."

"I can understand that," I whispered.

He was quiet for several moments. "You look so tired," he said. I didn't take offense. "Have you been having nightmares?"

"Tonight was the first," I admitted. "And I haven't had any more hallucinations."

"It's no surprise that you have nightmares. I have them." There was truth in his eyes when my gaze lifted to his. "Let me stay with you tonight. I know nightmares won't find either of us tonight if we're together."

My lips parted. "Caden—"

"Let me lay beside you so both of us can sleep peacefully. That's all I want. No expectations. No conversations," he said—pleaded, really. "Let me be here for you tonight."

I knew I needed to say no. This had *bad idea* written all over it, even if all he did was lay beside me, and I honestly didn't expect him to try anything else. Sleeping together was far too intimate. It would mean too much, and it would make distancing myself from him even harder.

But Caden had nightmares too, and no matter how much I wanted to harden my heart, I couldn't. I nodded, knowing I would regret this later, then lay down on my back.

"Thank you," he whispered. Those two words entrenched themselves in my skin.

Caden toed off his shoes and without wasting a moment, turned off the light and then climbed into bed beside me. I might've stopped breathing a little. I felt him even though he didn't touch me, and when I worked up the nerve to look in his direction, I found him lying on his side facing me, eyes closed. I could make out the shape of his hand resting beside his chest, on the bed. I closed my eyes, and after several moments, I rolled onto my side. As if my hand had a mind of its own, it moved beside his, and then I fell asleep.

No more nightmares found me.

Chapter 8

My house looked like it had when I left.

Gray-and-white-checkered throw pillows were fluffed and placed at the corners of the couch. A stack of books was piled neatly on the coffee table. Several tiny stuffed mice had been collected and left by a foyer table where all the mail had been placed. A pair of sandals sat on the bottom step of the staircase leading upstairs. Above them were black and white sneakers that belonged to Tink. The kitchen was utterly spotless, which was almost impossible with Tink living here.

My gaze flickered over the living room. This was where Aric had grabbed me. He'd been waiting for me, and I'd walked right in, having no idea that he was here. I knew that if I closed my eyes, I would hear his voice.

I hear you've been looking for me.

I didn't close my eyes, but his voice was still like a whisper in my ear.

"I tried to keep things the way you had them." Ivy had moved ahead of me, her long, curly red hair pulled up in a messy topknot. "I even dusted."

"Actually, it was me who dusted," Ren said, coming down the stairs. He'd quietly gone up there when we entered, and I knew he was scoping out the rooms, making sure no one was here.

Ivy rolled her eyes. "But I was the one who gave him the supplies."

"It was a joint effort then." I ran my hand along the back of the couch. "Thanks, you guys. I had no idea what to expect when I returned."

"It was no problem at all." Ivy looked down as Dixon pranced out from the kitchen, rubbing against her legs. Bending, she scratched him behind his ear.

Ren leaned against the banister of the stairs. "You sure you're ready to be back here?"

"More than ready." I forced a smile that felt as fake as pleather.

The two of them exchanged a look, and I knew they had questions. Lots of them.

Luce had checked me over this morning, and after setting up a time for me to visit her the following weekend, she'd cleared me to leave Hotel Good Fae. I'd expected Tink to show up then, but come to find out, he was already at the house with Fabian and Dixon. It was Ivy and Ren who arrived as Luce left. All I knew was that Caden had asked them to escort me home, but I had no idea what, if anything, he'd said to them.

He'd been gone when I woke up, but that didn't change the fact that I'd gotten the deepest sleep I had in a really long time. Neither had it erased the moments at dawn when, still mostly asleep, I felt the bed shift and the soft sensation of his lips against my forehead. I told myself repeatedly that had been my imagination.

"Well, if you need anything, you know you got us," Ren said as Dixon meandered over to me, the white tip of his gray tail swishing. "And even if you don't need us, you still have us."

"We'll be making periodic patrols," Ivy said. They'd been filled in about the traitor in the Summer Court, but as discussed, they hadn't been told everything.

"Your phone is on the kitchen counter," Ivy explained while Dixon stretched up, pressing tiny paws into my legs. I picked him up, burying my face in his soft fur as Ivy said, "Oh, and by the way, Miles said to call him whenever you're ready or stop by the headquarters."

Face still planted in Dixon's fur, I nodded. "He most likely wants to see if I'm mentally stable and find out if I spilled any Order secrets."

"He didn't *exactly* suggest that, but…" Ivy trailed off.

I cracked a grin. Miles was the bluntest and most deadpan person I'd ever met. Even more so than Faye. Not one to beat around the bush, his first concern would be if I shared any of the Order's secrets.

"He should be happy to know that Aric didn't seem to care at all about the Order," I told them as Dixon purred.

"Actually, that would probably displease him," Ren commented.

I snorted at that and lifted my head, looking around the sundrenched room. "How did he respond to the news about there being someone in the Summer Court who's working with the Winter fae?"

"The same way Miles takes the news about almost everything," Ivy answered. "He raised his brows, was silent for probably a good minute, and then said something like 'there's always one rotten apple in the bunch.'"

"That sounds like him," I said dryly. "I almost wish we didn't have to tell him, but the members need to be on their toes."

"Agreed." Ren folded his arms. "It's not like every Order member has dropped their guard around the Summer fae, but they have relaxed, and that could be deadly."

And that was why the Order members needed to know.

"I just don't get how any of them could do that." Ivy shook her head, causing a thick curl to fall over one eye. "Them supporting the Queen's return is bad enough, but to aid the Winter Court when they're using stuff like Devil's Breath to destroy the younglings? It just doesn't make sense."

It really didn't. "Aric had said that whoever it was had their reasons. I don't think he said more. Or if he did, I...I don't remember it. But you're right, it doesn't make sense."

"I feel like we're missing something," Ren said. "I've been thinking about this, and I can't come up with a reason a Summer fae would want the Winter Queen to enter this world, especially since they have their bright and shiny King."

A small grin tugged at my lips.

"It's not like they're without leadership or whatever. So, the only thing that makes any sense to me is that it's someone who has a vendetta against the King and would rather risk the whole world to either see him taken out or returned to his former evil glory."

My heart turned over heavily at the thought. "But what kind of vendetta could drive a Summer fae to these extremes? If Caden were somehow placed under the Queen's curse again, they'd have an even bigger problem on their hands."

"So, maybe they were hoping Aric or the Queen would kill Caden," Ivy suggested, and my stomach dipped. "Take him out so another could become King."

I frowned as I thought that over. "From what I understand, only he can be King since he accepted the crown...or whatever. That even if he abdicated the throne, Fabian wouldn't become King. The Court would be without a ruler, but I have no idea what would happen if Caden died." The last word tasted like ash on my tongue.

"That might be a good question to ask," Ren said. "But I doubt we'll get an answer out of Fabian. He'd probably suspect that we were plotting to murder his brother."

"I could ask," I volunteered.

Ivy looked over her shoulder in the direction of the side door that led to the courtyard. "I hate to even ask this, but we don't believe that Fabian has any desire to be King, do we?"

"No. I don't believe that he does," I said honestly as Dixon rubbed his nose against my shoulder. "There are...certain expectations that I don't think Fabian has any desire to fulfill."

Neither did Caden, but that was neither here nor there.

"But why would anyone want to remove Caden as King?" Ivy asked, lips pursed. "I mean, he seems to be doing an okay job, and it isn't like he's unfair or cruel."

She was right, but I didn't think Caden wanted to be King before he took on the role. He'd felt forced, and that was before things really escalated between us. Even now, he was willing to shirk his obligations, but no one knew that while I had been held captive by Aric. And those who now knew about him ending his engagement were the only fae I one hundred percent trusted.

So maybe the traitor's motivations had nothing to do with Caden? If so, that brought us all the way back to square one. Why would a Summer fae work with the Winter Court?

For some reason, I thought of the old leader of the Order. David Cuvillier had betrayed the Order by aiding the Winter Court and Queen. He'd done so out of fear and resignation, believing that we hadn't stood a chance against the Winter Court. Could the traitor within the Summer Court have a similar mentality?

Fear could make some brave.

But fear could also turn others into the worst kind of cowards.

Chapter 9

"Are Fabian and Tink still out in the courtyard?" Ivy asked, drawing me from my unsettled thoughts.

Ren nodded. "Yeah, I have no idea what they're doing. I should probably go annoy them."

Smiling slightly, I watched him walk toward the kitchen, stopping to tip Ivy's head back and brush a kiss across her lips.

A pang of jealousy and envy stabbed me, and I reburied my face in Dixon's fur. He purred louder, like a little engine. After a few moments, I became aware of Ivy moving closer. I looked up, not at all surprised to see the concern in her gaze.

"I want to ask if everything is okay, but I know that's a stupid question. So, I'll try to refrain from asking that," she said, coming to stand beside me. "How are you feeling being back here, though?"

"It's…it's good, but it is weird," I admitted, thinking that if anyone knew what it felt like, it was Ivy. She had been through her own messed-up abduction. "Like it almost seems surreal to be here."

She nodded in understanding. "When I was taken, there were times when I didn't think I'd ever see my apartment again or the people I cared about. The first day home was a weird one."

There had been many moments when I didn't think I was going to walk out of that nightmare.

"Ren and Tink being there for me helped. If they hadn't been, I probably would've eventually dealt with everything, but having them made it easier." She scratched Dixon's ear as she lifted her gaze to mine. "Can I give you some unsolicited advice? Don't shut out the people who want to help."

"I'm not."

Her brows arched.

I sighed. "Things are complicated right now. That's all I want to say about it."

"You don't have to say anything," Ivy responded. "Just remember that I'm here when and if you do."

"I will," I promised.

Eventually, Ren returned inside with Tink and Fabian. It was hard to look at Caden's brother and not see the impossible similarities in the golden hair and cut of Fabian's jaw. After a bit, Ren and Ivy left, and Dixon found his way to Tink. Somehow, and I wasn't even sure how, I ended up on the couch, squished between Tink and Fabian and buried under a small mountain of blankets. There were no questions about how I was feeling or what was going on. Tink turned on what had to be his favorite movie, oblivious to Fabian's long-suffering sigh. *Twilight.* At this point, I'd seen it a hundred times, and I could recite those lines right alongside Tink, but I wasn't complaining. Well, I would draw the line at *Breaking Dawn.* That whole plot would hit way too close to home at the moment. Pizza was ordered for lunch, and since I'd been given the all-clear to eat whatever, I might've gone a bit overboard and eaten half of the pies. For once, Tink didn't comment, but I could tell he was bursting at the seams to make a comment about how I was now eating for two, though was doing his best to keep his mouth shut.

I'd relaxed between them, and by the start of *Eclipse*, I dozed on and off. I didn't know what made me think of the community in Florida, but a plan formed in my mind, one that might actually work.

The moment Fabian left, I twisted toward Tink, who had been combing Dixon's fur. "How big is the fae community in Florida? Is it like Hotel Good Fae?"

"Bigger, I think. There are several thousand there, and they don't stay in a hotel or use glamour to hide where they live. They have several gated subdivisions that are all together, built right by a beach. Super smart what they did by gating the communities." He dragged the small comb down Dixon's back. "Makes the beaches sort of private since you have to come in through the gates. People just think those who live in there are super rich or something."

"Do any humans live there?"

He nodded. "Some of the fae there are in relationships with humans."

That was good. "Did you like it there?"

Tink shrugged as he glanced at the screen as Jacob went full wolf. "I liked it."

"What about Fabian? He normally lives there, right? Does he plan to go back?"

"I think so, eventually." He frowned. "Do you ever wonder why Bella couldn't just have both Jacob and Edward?"

"What?"

"I mean, Edward has been alive for a while, so he's gotta get bored with the same old, same old. And Jacob is a wolf. I'm sure both have seen and done stranger things," he reasoned. "Plus, sharing is caring."

I stared at him and then gave a shake of my head. "No, I've never thought about that."

"You have boring thoughts then."

I ignored that. "Do you think I could go there? To the community in Florida?"

He returned to combing Dixon, focusing on his tail. "Why would you want to do that?"

"I could use the vacation."

Tink glanced at me. "You probably could."

"And…" I took a deep breath. "If Caden doesn't end up picking a Queen soon, I'm eventually going to start showing. It won't be easy to hide."

"Wait a second." Dropping the comb beside him, Tink picked up the remote and paused the movie. He looked at me. "You want to go down to the community to basically hide."

"And to relax. I have enough money saved up, and I'm sure Miles would—"

"You want to go hide in a fae community while becoming obviously pregnant?"

"No one down there should know who I am, right? It's not like Fabian or you told any random fae that I was the human chick the King was hooking up with."

"Of course not. Although, that would've been juicy gossip. But do you really think Fabian isn't going to know who the baby daddy is?"

I opened my mouth.

"He's not going to believe for one second that anyone but his brother is the father," he said before I could speak. "So, you'd be putting him in a position where he'll have to either knowingly lie to his brother or betray you."

I snapped my mouth shut. Shit. "I didn't think about that."

"Obviously."

"I really hadn't." I sank into the couch, surprised that I had forgotten that very important detail. "It's like my brain isn't fully functional or something."

"I just think you're really desperate, and desperate people do and think stupid things."

"Gee, thanks."

Tink was still for a bit and then placed Dixon in my lap. "Can I be honest for a moment?"

I slid him a sideways glance. "I have a feeling you were just super honest right then."

"I'm about to be even more honest. Like really super honest. The realest real kind of honesty."

"I think I get it."

"But you don't." He tipped toward me as Dixon sat up in my lap, watching him. "I get why you're doing what you are. I do. You want to save the world and some shit. Honorable. I'm not going to mess up your need to martyr your warm and fuzzies."

"It's not my need—"

"But it's become clear to me that you really are delusional."

"Wow," I murmured.

"Why else would you think your idea to hide with your baby daddy's brother in a community of fae was good enough to interrupt *Eclipse*? But it's more than that. Do you honestly think Caden is going to marry someone else even if he believes you don't want him?"

My stomach dropped. "He has to."

"He doesn't have to do jack shit, Lite Bright. I feel like everyone, including Tanner and Faye, is forgetting that. He didn't want to be King in the first place, and the last I checked, he's a grown-ass adult. Besides in the highly unlikely event that he's going to be like 'YOLO, let me pick a fae Queen now,' do you really think he's just going to let you walk away? Not fight for you? And I don't mean that in a creepy, super-possessive way either, but in a way we all would want someone we cared about to fight for us."

All the pizza I'd shoved down my throat was starting to settle wrongly in my stomach.

"But I have a really important question for you. One you need to think about long and hard before answering," he went on. "Do you honestly think you're going to be able to shut down the way you feel about him? You're going to be able to stand by and watch him be with someone else? You're going to be able to resist him—resist what you want—when he *does* fight for you?"

* * * *

I hadn't answered Tink's question, and he hadn't expected one, but I had thought about it. I'd spent the rest of the day and a good part of that night thinking about it, and every time I said that, yes, I could resist all of Caden's attempts, there was a little laugh in the back of my mind.

But what other choice did I have?

Restless after downing a glass of orange juice and a small army's worth of eggs, I took the prenatal vitamin and roamed upstairs, my head in a really weird place.

Slowly, I went down the hall of the second floor, past the closed door of the office, beyond the room Tink had commandeered, and to the other closed door—the one my mother had used.

I could use her room for the baby. My stomach wiggled like it always did whenever I acknowledged being pregnant. That was if I was still here then. The community in Florida was a stupid idea, but there were a million other places. If I was here, though, the room would be large, but since the small one that had once been a nursery had been converted into a walk-in closet ages ago, it was the only option. Well, unless Tink ever moved out. His room was smaller. Maybe he'd want the larger one?

Pushing open my bedroom door, I halted just inside the threshold. Last night, I hadn't really paid attention when I climbed into bed, too caught up in my thoughts. Now, I cataloged every square inch as if looking for something to be different. The drapes had been parted, letting in the morning sunlight. The velvety-soft cream bedspread had been smoothed back from the thick pillows. A pair of slippers I always left out but rarely wore waited by the bed. A fluffy and chunky gray throw blanket was draped over the chair by the window. It looked and felt the same. The room even smelled like I remembered. Like pineapple and mango.

But *I* wasn't the same.

My gaze made its way to the closet. I forced my steps forward. Opening the closet door, I switched on the light. What I saw first were the wigs in various colors and lengths, the knee-high boots and spiky heels, and the skintight dresses. They were all costumes designed to hide my identity while I hunted the fae responsible for killing my mother. I didn't need them anymore. I'd succeeded. They were all dead now, and those wigs and dresses...

They'd become a part of who and what I'd been shaped into. I ran my hand over the Lycra material of a red dress that I wouldn't have dared to wear five years ago. The outfits, the wigs, the shoes—all had aided me in finding the fae responsible for killing my mother, but they'd also done something else. They'd given me the confidence I'd been sorely lacking.

But this stuff still wasn't me. They were words written in blood and tears for a chapter that had come to an end.

Pivoting around, I hurried downstairs to the pantry. Black garbage bags in hand, I went back to the closet and started cleaning house. Everything went. The wigs. The shoes. The dresses—well, *almost* everything. I couldn't bear to part with the studded mid-calf boots or the silvery sequined dress. Those boots were surprisingly comfortable, and the dress...

It was the outfit I'd been wearing when I killed Tobias—one of the fae I'd been looking for.

And it was the dress I had on the first time I came face-to-face with Caden in the club.

For that reason alone, I should toss it with the rest, but I hung it back up between the thick, oversized cardigan and the blazer I never wore.

Pulling open the drawers in the center dresser, I breathed a sigh of relief when I spotted the extra sets of iron daggers and cuffs. I closed the drawer and then picked up my makeup case. Setting it on the counter inside the closet, I flipped the switches and rooted around, pulling out the heavier makeup—the stuff I wouldn't even wear for a fancy occasion.

Not that I attended many fancy things.

I dumped the makeup into an old grocery bag and walked out—

Caden stood in the doorway of the bedroom, arms loosely crossed over the plain gray tee shirt he wore as he stared at the garbage bags.

He lifted his chin, and the room seemed to tilt as our gazes connected. His hair was pulled back, and the beams of sunlight seemed to be attracted to all the striking, symmetrical angles and planes of his face.

Upon the unexpected sight, my heart lodged itself in my throat. Now, it was firmly back in my chest, pounding for reasons unrelated to shock.

Caden was...he was gorgeous, his beauty rugged and raw. As shallow as this sounded, I could stare at him all day, and there was a good chance he knew that. Warmth crept into my cheeks and flowed down my throat. It took a moment for me to find my ability to speak. "How did you get in here?"

One side of his lips quirked up. "You know I'm not a vampire, right? I don't need permission to enter a home."

My eyes narrowed. "I'm pretty sure the front door was locked."

"It was."

I lifted my brows.

"Tink let me in," he answered finally, eyes twinkling.

I really needed to talk to Tink about letting Caden in. Not like this was the first time, but that damn brownie knew better.

He unfolded his arms, the act doing interesting things to the muscles under his shirt. "Doing some light spring cleaning?"

"Something like that."

"What are you going to do with all that stuff?"

I glanced down at the overflowing bags. "I thought I'd give them to Goodwill or a women's shelter." My nose scrunched. "Although, they'd probably wonder if an escort had cleaned out their closet."

"A high-priced escort," Caden murmured, and my lips twitched at that. "I have to say I'm glad to see you throwing this stuff away."

I almost said that I didn't care what he felt, but doing so would lessen the significance of what getting rid of these items meant.

"Although…" He reached inside a bag and pulled out a knee-high boot that took an act of God to get off. "I will miss these."

Storming forward, I snatched the boot from his hands and dropped it back into the bag. Caden grinned down at me as if greatly amused by my actions. My stomach did a little flip, and I was reminded of Tink's question. Could I resist Caden?

"What made you do this?" He gestured at the bags with his chin.

I backed up, crossing my arms. Like always, it was almost impossible not to open up. I had no idea why it was like that with him. "They're costumes—the clothing, the wigs, all of it. I don't need them anymore."

"No more late-night visits to clubs then?"

A picture of me in a skintight dress, several months pregnant, formed in my mind, and I snorted. "Not in the foreseeable future."

"What about patrolling?"

That was a good question. "The Order never really had me patrolling, but I…I like being out there." How long I would be able to do that safely was anyone's guess. "I just won't be looking for any fae in particular, I guess."

His jaw tightened as if he weren't all that happy to hear that I still planned to patrol, but he wisely didn't voice his opinion.

In the ensuing silence, I looked at the bags. "Everything that's in those bags isn't me, you know? They really were like costumes, and I don't need them anymore."

"I'm glad to hear that," he replied. "They represent a chapter of your life that's now closed."

I blinked in surprise as he nailed how I felt. He really did know me. Better than anyone else. Panic blossomed in the pit of my stomach, and my mouth dried. "Why are you here, Caden? I know last night might've confused things, but I'm sure I made myself clear."

"Oh, you were clear, all right."

"Then should I repeat my question?"

"If it makes you feel better? Sure. Go ahead."

"It wouldn't make me feel better."

"Good. Because I don't want you feeling bad." He stepped forward, and I tensed. That reaction had nothing to do with my time with Aric. "I want you to feel good. I want you happy. I want you to feel safe and cherished. I want you to feel comforted and comfortable. I want you to feel loved."

Oh God.

All those broken shards of my heart started to piece themselves back together. I needed them to stop. A repaired heart would only hurt worse.

Caden took another step forward, and I moved until the backs of my legs hit the bed. "Did you sleep well last night? I did. Best sleep I've had in years, sunshine."

My heart jumped. *Sunshine.* He called me that because he said he'd seen me smiling once and it was like the sun finally rising. That was possibly the sweetest, kindest thing anyone had ever said to me.

"It's time."

I looked up. "For what?"

"For that talk I told you we needed to have but would be better if we waited until you had time to process everything you'd gone through. But I can see we don't have the luxury of that time," he said. "I know, Brighton."

My breath caught. "Know what?"

Those golden eyes met and held mine. "I *know.*"

Chapter 10

My legs seemed to have given up on me because I was suddenly sitting on the edge of the bed.

He…he knew?

How?

Well, there were countless hows. Four of them had a name. I didn't believe Tink had said anything about me being pregnant, but the other three could've just been convincing when they'd said they wouldn't say anything.

"Know what?" I repeated.

His head tilted to the side like it did whenever he was sensing some sort of emotion I was giving off. I was sure he was picking up on them.

"I know you've been told what would happen if I do not marry Tatiana or a fae of the Court," he said.

My mouth opened as my heart pressed against my ribs. Relief made me dizzy, so much so that I almost laughed. He didn't know. Not really.

His head tipped to the side once again, and I knew I needed to get a handle on my emotions. I dragged my hands over my bent knees, knowing there was no point in lying about what I'd learned. "You mean the basic collapse of your Court and how you'd be dethroned and left to fend for yourself? How the Summer fae would be weakened, and it would eventually lead to the whole world going to hell? How *you* would be weakened?"

Caden's features softened as I spoke, causing warning bells to go off left and right. "I'm honored, sunshine."

I blinked.

He came forward, each step slow and measured. "You don't need to worry about what will happen to me. I'm not worried."

"That's easy for you to say," I replied. "And also concerning that you're not worried."

Caden sat down, his large frame seeming to overwhelm the bed. "I will be fine, with or without the throne. But I won't be fine without you."

My heart gave a happy little jump, and I closed my eyes. "I wish you wouldn't say things like that."

"Why?" His voice was quiet.

"Because it's always so perfect. It's always what I..." It was what I wanted to hear, and that was the problem. "I just wish you wouldn't say things like that."

"I don't think you'd prefer that I lie."

Actually, I would in this situation.

"This is why you've tried to push me away," he said, and my eyes opened on the word *tried*. He was staring down at me, a slight smile on his lips. "It's not because you don't want me. It's not because you don't love me. It's because you think you're doing the right thing."

"Because I am," I snapped.

The smile grew. "Not that I needed the confirmation that I am right, but thank you nonetheless for providing it."

"It doesn't matter if you're right or wrong." I rose, shaking my head. "It doesn't matter how I feel or how you feel."

"It does matter that you believe you're doing the right thing. That you're *willing* to do the right thing. At least to me." He looked up at me, gaze warm. "You know what that says about you?"

"Yes. I'm brave or selfless or whatever." I waved a hand, dismissing that. "I'd rather be selfish."

"But never a coward?"

I didn't even have to consider the answer. "No."

"I didn't think so." His gaze searched mine. "I'm going to ask you something, Brighton, and I want you to be honest. I *need* you to be honest. Do you love me?"

Tension settled on my shoulders as I started to speak—to lie. But he already knew the truth. I imagined he just wanted to hear me say it. Either way, I didn't think I had it in me to force that lie past my lips once more.

"I love you, Caden." My voice thickened as I crossed my arms and gripped my waist. "I think...I think I fell in love with you the moment you walked into Flux and let me pretend I was under the glamour of a fae. I know that sounds weird, but I've always been able to tell you things I couldn't share with anyone else. As crazy as this sounds, I'm comfortable with you in a way I've never been with any guy, even though you're freaking perfect, and I'm the exact opposite of that. You're smart. You're funny, even when you're annoying the ever-loving crap out of me. You're sensitive in a way I don't think many people would ever expect you to be. So, yes, I love you, Caden."

His eyes closed briefly. When they reopened, it was almost like twin fires had lit them from within. "Do you know that the fae believe that a piece of their soul is released upon birth and finds a home in their soulmate?"

Recalling what Luce had said about two souls and the *mortuus*, I had a feeling that whatever he was about to say was going to make me cry.

"I found that piece of my soul in Siobhan. When she was killed, I didn't believe that I would ever find it again, even though the fae believe that upon death, that piece of the soul is once more released. You see, I was lucky when I found Siobhan. Not all fae find the missing piece of their soul. It doesn't mean that their love for another is any less real. It's just that two souls being connected is more intense and immediate. It can happen with just one look." He pressed his palm against his chest. "What is in here recognizes what belongs. The joining of two souls is an unbreakable bond."

A tremor coursed through me as I fought the urge to both run to him and run from the room.

"I saw you before the night the gateways to the Otherworld were sealed. Just brief glimpses, but each time, I felt this throbbing in my chest. It had been so long since I'd felt anything like it that I wasn't sure what I was feeling. But that night when you helped my brother..." His voice roughened as he tipped forward. "I knew that somehow, someway, the part of my soul that had been released had found another home. I never would've dared to hope I'd find you, the one who held a piece of my soul, but I did."

What he said would've sounded crazy to me a handful of years ago. Soulmates? I would've said they only existed in fairy tales. But now? This made sense.

"I tried to stay away then. I could sense your fear and distrust of the fae, and when I realized that you could be used against me like Siobhan had been, I tried to distance myself from you. Both were mistakes, ones I will spend an eternity trying to make up for."

A breath seemed to shudder out of him. "I love you, Brighton. I know I fell in love with you before we even spoke to one another. That love only deepened when I saw how strong and resilient you became.

When I learned how incredibly intelligent and generous you are."

The back of my throat and eyes burned as he continued. "My love for you grew each time you pushed back at me, showing me you weren't afraid, and I knew the reason why you became my *mortuus* when you were willing to look past who I was and saw beyond what I'd done when I was under the Queen's spell. You are my sun, Brighton. I loved you before I found you in that club, even before I gave you the Summer Kiss."

I shuddered, taking a step back. "Caden…" I pushed the tears down. "What you just said, it was beautiful, and I know it's real. There is something entirely inexplicable about us. But hearing that…it hurts."

"It's not meant to hurt, sunshine. I wish you would've come to me the moment you heard what would happen if I didn't choose a Queen. I think I could've saved you a lot of heartache."

I wasn't sure how hearing this days ago would've lessened the amount of pain I was in.

"What if I told you that you could be selfish?" he asked.

Letting out a dry laugh, I shook my head again. "Caden, it's not like I haven't thought about this. About whether either of us could live with ourselves, knowing what we've risked. I know I can't. I know you couldn't."

"I didn't want to be King. You know that," he said. "But that doesn't mean I would let my Court rot and decay."

"See?" I reasoned. "You agree. We can't be together. No matter how badly we want to be. So, this conversation is only hurting both of us."

"This was a conversation I planned to have once you had a little time to process everything you've been through and learned," he repeated. "Because what I'm about to tell you will come as another shock, but I see now waiting was a mistake. Sometimes we think we're doing the right thing when we're not."

Considering what I knew that he didn't, I doubted he could shock me. "What do you have to tell me?"

"I have to tell you that I have chosen a Queen."

My entire body jerked as my heart twisted painfully in my chest. I searched desperately for relief but found nothing but aching emptiness and bitterness. This was what the world needed, but God, it still cut so deeply. "Okay," I whispered, wondering what the hell the point of this conversation was. "Congrats."

One side of his lips curved up. "Perhaps I need to be a bit clearer. I've chosen you, Brighton. I've chosen you to be my Queen."

Chapter 11

"Me?" I squeaked. I couldn't have heard him right. There was no way.

Caden nodded. "You. I've chosen you."

I stared at him for what felt like an eternity, heart racing, and stomach feeling as if I were poised at the top of a rollercoaster. "You can't choose me."

"Oh, yes, I can," he replied. "And I have."

"But the Summer Court, the world—"

"Will be just fine." He reached out, curling his fingers around my elbows. "Because you are my *mortuus,* and I've given you the Summer Kiss."

"What does that have to do with it?" Tears blurred his face.

"Because you're not entirely human any longer." He rose slowly as if trying not to startle me. "You're not fae, either. You have a piece of my soul inside you. That places you above any fae my Court could offer me. The Summer fae would not weaken, nor would the human world. I would not be dethroned." His thumbs slid along my elbows. "I would be whole."

Confusion swamped me as a tiny kernel of something more powerful than hope formed. Some fae knew I was Caden's *mortuus*—Tanner and Luce. I imagined Fabian knew, as did Tink. I didn't think any of them would be particularly dishonest with me. "Is this something well known? That your *mortuus,* no matter if they are fae or human, can be your Queen?"

"It's not just the *mortuus.* It's also the Summer Kiss," he explained, his gaze questioning. "Why?"

"I…" I'd told no one about the Summer Kiss. Luce didn't even know that. Neither did Tanner. Had Caden told Fabian? If so, he must've kept it from Tink because Tink would've told me. The tiny kernel grew, unfurling like a blossoming flower. "Are you…are you for real?"

"Why wouldn't I be?" Caden dragged his hands up my arms.

My brain sort of shorted out. I could have him and the future I wanted so badly and not risk the entire world? We could be together. Our child would have a mother and father who loved each other. My legs started to tremble, and I jerked back from his hold. "Why didn't you tell me this when you told me you ended your engagement with Tatiana!"

"Looking back, I realize I should have, but I figured you'd been through enough, and it seemed like a good idea to wait before I told you I planned to make you my wife. I figured after you had some time to heal, we'd talk," he explained. "I didn't expect anyone to go to you."

My breath came in short, quick pants. What he was saying sounded reasonable. He'd been thinking of what I could handle given that I'd just been held—wait. "You…you want to marry me?"

His lips twitched. "To make you my Queen, I would have to marry you."

"Is this a proposal?"

He grinned then, somehow looking boyish. "I had planned on doing something romantic."

Feeling like I might faint, I pressed my palm to the center of my chest. "You're not lying to me now, right?"

"I would not lie about this." He lifted his hands, cupping my cheeks. I didn't flinch. Everything that had happened with Aric was the furthest thing from my mind. "I would never lie to you about how I feel or our future. Never again, sunshine."

"This isn't…this isn't a hallucination, is it?"

Anguish filled his gaze. "No, sunshine. This is real."

I didn't know what happened next.

It was like a seal deep inside me cracked wide open. I tried to say his name, but all that came up was a deep, soul-shaking sob. The tears I'd been fighting overwhelmed me. Vaguely, I was aware of Caden gathering me in his arms, and then we were on the bed, him sitting with me in his lap, one arm wrapped tightly around me, a hand curled around the back of my head.

And I cried.

It was the ugly kind of crying that shook the entire body. Whatever had been ripped open inside of me had been a Pandora's box of emotions. What spilled out of me was a mixture of the best and the worst of the storm. Some of the tears that fell were for all the wounds Aric had caused, those inflicted years ago, the ones that had faded, and the ones that were never visible. The death of my mother, the way I never felt truly valued by the Order, and even the loss of the father I'd never known fueled the sobs. But there was a different side to the outpouring of emotion as well. A wealth of relief and such potent happiness that all I could do was cry. And I never happy-cried.

But I was now because I didn't have to watch the man I loved bind his life to someone else. I wouldn't have to walk away, knowing I would never feel the kind of love I had for him again, nor would I ever have to worry if I'd find someone who loved me as much as he did. I didn't have to hide our child from him. He could be a part of the child's life from the beginning. We wouldn't have that house with the white picket fence, but we would have each other.

We would have a future together. That realization made me cry even harder, and the whole time, Caden held me. He whispered words to me that reminded me of music. It was a language I couldn't begin to understand. Still, it soothed all the frayed edges until finally the tears subsided, and the tremors stopped.

There was so much I wanted to tell him as I lifted my head from his chest. There was so much I needed to tell him as I looked up and saw the concern in his gaze as he dragged his hand around to my cheek. That I was pregnant. That he was about to become a father. That I loved him. That I now believed in soulmates. That the tears weren't all bad. That happy couldn't even begin to describe the hope, anticipation, excitement, and the hundred other emotions I currently felt.

But as Caden's thumb dragged over my lower lip, I knew that if he felt one-tenth of the rawness swirling around inside me, now wasn't the time for words. Fire replaced the concern in his gaze, and the way his lips parted and his chest rose sharply against my hands was intentional. Tension poured into the air around us, becoming a tangible third entity. I imagined I could almost see the air heating and crackling. A heavy ache settled in my breasts and then moved lower, between my thighs. It was a deep, pulsing throb that I didn't just welcome but reveled in because it was more than just primal physical attraction. It was our love for one another manifesting into something that could not be denied.

Time for words would come later.

Closing the distance between us, I kissed Caden. The touch of his lips against mine was a jolt to the system. It was like brushing up against a live wire, lighting up the network of nerves all across my body. I shuddered as the arm around me tightened, drawing me against the hot, hard length of his body. The taste of him against my lips, on my tongue, was like ambrosia. Every part of me became hyperaware of how his mouth felt against mine, his lips soft yet hard. How he tasted like sunshine and summer against the tip of my tongue.

Giving in to the rising tide of sensations, I rocked my hips against him. The thin leggings I wore were no barrier to the hardness pressing against the material of his jeans. He skated his fingers through my hair, his hand balling in the loose strands. A deep, growling sound radiated out from the back of his throat and rumbled through me. The tips of my breasts tingled, and the kiss went deeper as he managed to hold me even tighter. A moan curled its way out of my throat as he shifted under me, lining his hips up perfectly with mine. My fingers dug into his shirt as my pulse became a heady thrum.

I almost whimpered as Caden broke the kiss, pulling back as his gaze roamed over my face. I didn't care what I looked like after having cried for the Lord knew how long, because I realized he didn't see the puffy eyes or tear-streaked cheeks or the remnants of the fading bruises and healing cuts.

He saw me.

Only *me*.

"Are you sure?" he whispered, his gaze searching mine intently. "Because we can do everything, or we don't have to do anything. I would be happy to just hold you, to just kiss and play, Brighton. I'm satisfied with you being in my arms."

Fresh tears pricked my eyes, but I didn't worry if they fell or not. "That is why I'm sure." His willingness to wait, to do nothing or anything was why I knew I was ready, why it wasn't too soon after everything that'd happened. "I need you, Caden. Make love to me. Please?"

"You never have to say please. Ever." Cradling my cheeks in his hands, he shuddered against me. "All that I am. All that I have. It's yours. I'm yours."

Caden kissed me then, and oh God, no one—*no one*—kissed like him. His mouth moved over mine like he was claiming every hidden part of my heart and soul. My shirt came off. Then his. We stood, our mouths and hands skimming over every inch of exposed skin. His fingers gripped the band of my leggings, tugging them down, along with the panties I wore underneath. I reached for the button on his jeans, hands trembling as I then worked at the zipper. Off went his pants, and then he eased down the tight, black boxer briefs he had on, freeing the rigid length of his cock.

Caden was…he was beautiful. Every part of him, from the broad expanse of his chest and the tightly rolled muscles of his stomach, to the proud jut of his arousal.

So distracted by the sight of him, I hadn't even noticed that he'd unclasped my bra until his mouth closed over one nipple. I cried out, reaching for those silky strands of hair, but he dropped to his knees in front of me.

His lips brushed over the faint pink scars from two years ago. "Beautiful." He tilted his head, kissing one of the many almost-healed slices. "You're so beautiful, Brighton. Every part of you." He sank even lower, his lips searching and tasting, licking and exploring until his breath danced over my most sensitive area. Then his head shifted, and I felt the wet slide of his tongue along my inner thigh, moving up and up until it slipped inside, swirling and tasting. Each time his tongue thrust in, pleasure became a lightning bolt down my spine. "This is especially beautiful."

His mouth closed over the bundle of nerves, and my head fell back. There was no slow build of sensation. He knew exactly what he was doing when he dragged his teeth over my sensitive skin, soothing the bite with his tongue before closing his mouth over the turgid flesh. The release hit me hard. Crying out, my head fell back as pounding wave after wave of pleasure roared through me.

Before the tremors stopped, Caden rose. Somehow, we ended up on the bed, his large body settling over mine and then between my thighs. His mouth found mine once more, and the taste of me mingled with the essence of him.

"I waited several lifetimes for you," he said, brushing the hair back from my face. "I would wait several more if I had to."

"You don't." I touched his cheeks and then slid my hand down the sides of his neck to his shoulders. "You don't have to wait anymore. I don't have to wait."

Caden's body shifted, and I felt him pressing against me. I lifted my hips, and my breath caught and then held. His gaze snared mine. "This feels like a dream. If it is, I don't ever want to wake…" His voice choked off as he thrust in, fully seating himself. The pressure and fullness was unbelievable, and the small bit of discomfort faded as he made a sound, a velvety growl. "Sunshine."

From there, there were only our short, shallow breaths and the sounds of our bodies moving together. His hips rolled and pumped, and I followed, the unbelievable tension building once more.

Caden planted his elbow in the bed beside my head as he shoved his arm under my back and lifted me so my breasts were pressed to his chest. His strength was shocking and wickedly arousing as he moved over me. In me. Each stroke deeper and harder, became more powerful. My back hit the mattress once more. I curled my legs around his waist, and I met each deep and even thrust until I couldn't any longer, until the pace quickened, and his body held mine down. My body tensed around his, and my blood turned to lava as every part of my body tightened at once, all over again.

"That's it." His voice was a heated whisper in my ear.

The most intense pleasure rolled over me in tight, hot waves, and all I could do was hold on as his hips pounded in a tempo that was earth-shattering. Our mouths crashed together His tongue tangled with mine, and the tightly coiled knot of tension whipped through me fiercely, lighting up every cell in my body.

The arm under my shoulders held me in place as he ground his hips into mine. There was one more deep, breath-shattering thrust, and then my name was a rough shout as his body spasmed, his release hot as his hips jerked. My hands glided lazily up and down his sides as one last shudder overtook him.

Caden's lips brushed over my shoulder and then the line of my jaw. Limp and sated, I watched him through half-open eyes. His hand found mine, and he brought it to his mouth, pressing a kiss to the center of my palm. "I have a very important question for you, Brighton."

"Hmm?"

He brought my hand to his chest, over his heart. "Can we stay like this for the rest of the day?"

A slow grin tugged at my lips. "Like *this*?" I asked. He was still inside me, not as hard as he had been, but not remotely soft.

Biting down on his bottom lip, he nodded. "What about all weekend?"

"I would…I would be down for that." My heart was swelling so fast in my chest. "Though I don't think we can stay like this."

"I don't know." His hips rocked, eliciting a sharp gasp from me. His grin became downright wicked. "I'm quite happy to be right where I am."

I started to reach for him when, somewhere from the floor, a phone rang. I looked, brows furrowing. My phone was downstairs. "I think that's yours."

"It is." He bent his head, kissing me. The ringing quieted, and for a few seconds, I got a little lost in him, but then the cell started ringing again.

"I think you should check that."

"I should." Caden cursed under his breath. "Sorry."

"It's okay," I whispered.

Giving me one more quick kiss, he eased out of me and smoothly shifted to his feet. My gaze dropped to his ass as he snatched his jeans off the floor.

That was one lovely backside.

Feeling better than I had in, well, longer than I could remember, I rolled onto my side.

Caden had his phone out and to his ear, answering with an abrupt, "This better be important."

My brows rose, and I started to grin, but I saw the muscles along his back and spine tense. The pleasant languidness vanished.

"I'll be right there," he said, ending the call as he turned to me.

"What is it?"

"It's Benji, Faye's missing cousin. He came back to the hotel."

Sensing the hard edge to his voice, unease blossomed. "It didn't end with a happy reunion, did it?"

"No." The fire had dimmed in Caden's eyes. "He attacked."

Chapter 12

I was already sitting up, scanning the floor for my discarded clothing. "How bad is it?"

"Not as bad as it could've been, but he wounded some of the guards," he told me as he pulled on his briefs and jeans. "And he injured his mother pretty badly."

"Oh God," I whispered, pulling on my leggings. "I assume he's dead?"

"Surprisingly not." His gaze flickered over my chest, lingering in a way that caused warmth to creep into my cheeks. He picked up my bra. "Faye and Kalen were able to apprehend and contain him."

Shock flickered through me as I took the bra from him, quickly donning it. "Holy crap, that's huge, Caden. We may find out where they're getting the Devil's Breath since you guys checked Neal's bar and didn't find any evidence of it."

"It is huge," he agreed.

I pulled on the loose sweater and then shoved up the sleeves. "We just need to get Benji to talk."

"And that's going to be easier said than done." He pulled his shirt on over his head. "You remember how Elliot was."

I thought of the youngling. He'd been crazed, almost as if brainwashed by the Winter Court. "But we have to try."

Caden's gaze flicked to mine, and then he came forward, smoothing my hair back from my face. "You look so delectable right now."

I didn't need a mirror to know my hair looked like I'd been, well, rolling around in bed.

"But *we* don't have to do anything," he continued. "I want you to sit this one out. Stay here, and I'll come back to you as soon as I can."

My brows lifted. "You want me to just sit and wait for you?"

"You don't have to sit and wait, so to speak."

I narrowed my eyes as I stepped back, out of his reach. "Why do you want me to sit this out?"

He lowered his hand. "You're still recovering, Brighton. That's the only reason why."

Taking a deep, even breath, I reminded myself that he was coming from a place of concern, and there was no reason for my head to spin *Exorcist* style. "You took my word when I said I was ready earlier."

His head tilted slightly. "I did."

"And we just had pretty active sex," I said, proud that my cheeks didn't catch fire.

Caden's eyes heated though, and his voice roughened. "We did. I would've loved to do it again." He paused, his gaze sweeping over me. "And again."

A delicious little shiver danced over my skin, and it took me a second to get my mind back on track. "If I was ready for that, why wouldn't I be ready for a questioning?"

"You mean an interrogation."

"Whatever."

"What we did and what I'm about to do are two different things. You won't like what you see down in that room."

"I've seen some really grotesque interrogations carried out by the Order, Caden, but you're right," I replied. "What *we* are about to do will be a hell of a lot easier than what we just did."

"And what you guys just did was very loud and seemed very active." A voice came from the doorway—the open doorway. I turned, finding Tink standing there. "I definitely think Brighton is physically ready…for just about anything."

Oh my God.

"Dixon got scared," he continued. "He's hiding out under the coffee table right now. Traumatized by all the sexing going on."

I had no words.

"By the way, you guys left the door open," Tink explained.

My lips parted as I shot Caden a quick glance. He didn't seem at all perturbed by that fact. Meanwhile, I wanted to bury myself under the bed. How could we have been that distracted?

Well, I knew exactly how we were that distracted.

"I was kind of worried at first. The sounds were interesting." Tink grinned as my eyes widened. "Shouting. Crying. Moaning. A totally different kind of crying—"

"Oh my God, Tink. You can stop now," I exclaimed. "Seriously."

"What?" He lifted his hands. "I'm just happy you finally got some—"

Tink shouted as I picked up my flip-flop and winged it at his head. Caden chuckled, and I had half a mind to throw the other shoe at his face. He ended that thought with one smoldering, fond look.

"Come on," he said, his gaze light despite what had happened. "You need to find better shoes if you're coming with me."

Relieved that he wasn't going to try to keep me wrapped in a bubble, I nodded and started for the closet.

"How about these?" Caden asked.

I looked over my shoulder. He held one of the knee-high boots, all helpful like.

He winked at me. "I have such fond memories of these."

"I'm going to throw that boot at your head," I warned.

Caden grinned. "It would be worth it."

* * * *

Sitting in the front seat of Caden's SUV, with him behind the steering wheel, and Tink in the back seat, I still found it weirdly funny that Caden, the King of the Summer fae, drove. Shouldn't he have a driver or something?

Tracing the outline of the iron cuffs on my wrists that hid the daggers, I wondered if at some point, as the baby grew, I would have difficultly handling iron. I didn't think so since contact with my skin didn't mean contact with the baby, but I supposed that was something I needed to keep an eye on. Wishing there was a guide for expecting fae mothers who were also members of the Order, I wiggled my toes inside my black combat boots. Obviously, I hadn't put on the other boots.

They did, however, end up back in my closet instead of in the bag to donate. "*For later*," Caden had said, which had caused Tink to launch into a discussion about how dressing up kept his sex life lively—something Caden didn't want to hear since it involved his brother.

Tink kept catching my gaze in the rearview mirror, and each time, he raised his brows. I knew he had a lot of questions. I couldn't blame him for that, considering I'd tried to convince him to take me to Florida just hours before. There wasn't time for that at the moment.

There also hadn't been time for me to tell Caden I was pregnant. I had been okay with keeping the truth from him when I had a good reason to do so, but now that there was none, it was pecking away at me. Each passing minute was one more minute where he didn't know he was going to be a father.

How would he take it? I didn't know. He loved me, I knew that beyond a doubt. But even if I'd known from the moment I woke up that I could be his Queen and all would be as well as it was, everything was still new. There'd be no time for just him and me. It would always be him, me, and our child. Though I didn't think we needed the time to get to know each other or to become comfortable. The latter was already there, and it was…it was truly like we were two halves coming together. We may not know every little thing about one another, but we knew each other.

Wait.

I would be his Queen.

My stomach dipped as I stared out the window, the rows of homes and wrought iron fences nothing but a blur.

He hadn't made it super official, but no way in hell would I say no. We would marry, and I would be his wife. A Queen. Would I have like queenly duties? What would the queenly duties even be? I gave a little shake of my head. I needed to focus. Right now, none of that was exactly important. Dealing with it could come later. What we needed to deal with was Benji, and then afterward, I would tell Caden about the pregnancy.

I glanced over at Caden as we turned on South Peters, experiencing a weird little hitch in my chest. A part of me still couldn't believe that this was real—that we could be together.

Caden pulled around to the side of the rundown, brick and metal building that looked like something you'd see on one of those ghost hunters shows.

"This part is so cool." Tink gripped the back of my seat as he popped his head between the two.

Caden drove up to what appeared to be a loading dock for deliveries—two wide metal doors that were covered in splotches of rust— and then right *through* the doors. I didn't close my eyes, but I did tense. I'd entered Hotel Good Fae a few times like this, and it always freaked me out. I kept expecting to crash into a cement wall.

"Magic," Tink murmured in my ear.

"Uh-huh." My eyes adjusted to the fluorescent lighting of the parking garage.

He pulled into the first parking space near the elevator, one I was sure had been reserved for him. Killing the engine, Caden looked over at me, and his gaze met mine. There was a flutter in my chest and then my stomach. I smiled at him.

"Ready?" he asked, and I nodded. He glanced back at Tink. "You?"

"Why, thanks for asking." He sat back, looking between the two of us. "I am ready for some answers to the questions that have been burning me up inside, but with my dark hair comes great responsibility, and a newfound maturity."

I blinked slowly.

"So I realized that now is not the time to ask those questions." He held up his hand. "But as soon as you guys are done with what you're doing, I expect the three of us—no, wait. I'm sure Fabian would also like to be included. The four of us will have a sit-down."

"It's doable." Caden grinned.

"It is." I met Tink's gaze. "But it's going to have to wait a little bit. There's something I need to talk to Caden about first."

Tink's eyes widened, and I was grateful that I could feel Caden's gaze on me. "What do you need to talk to me about?" he said, drawing my gaze back to his. "We can make time now. Benji isn't going anywhere."

Out of the corner of my eye, I saw Tink clasp his hands together under his chin. There was no way I was telling Caden that he was going to be a father in front of Tink. That would be like going on a reality show.

"It can wait," I told him.

Caden's gaze searched mine, and then he nodded. Exhaling roughly, I ignored the pout Tink sent in my direction and climbed out. I didn't make it far before Tink curled an arm around my shoulders, pulling me against his side.

He lowered his head, whispering, "Is everything okay?"

"Everything is more than okay."

Tink pulled back, smiling. "I am going to need an extremely detailed report. You know that, right?"

I laughed. "I do."

"Good."

It was then that I realized Caden hadn't walked toward the elevator. He'd stopped halfway across the parking garage. Tink and I caught up with him. "Where are we going?"

"To a place where Tanner handles certain…unpleasantries."

This is the first I'm hearing of such a thing. I glanced at Tink, and he shrugged. "There is such a place?"

Caden nodded. "Only a few know of it. I'm surprised my brother didn't tell you."

Tink snorted as he shoved his hands into the pockets of his sweatpants. "He knows I abhor violence unless it's violence I'm causing."

I frowned at him as we reached a nondescript white door. Caden placed his thumb against the keypad, and above, the red light turned green. The door unlocked, and he pushed it open. We stepped into a white hallway, and I could already hear Tanner speaking. There were also other voices I couldn't make out. Caden turned to me, extending his hand.

My gaze dipped to his palm and then rose to his. He…he wanted to hold my hand? It was such a simple gesture that wouldn't mean much to others, but it would be huge.

He was the King.

To the others who were here, I was just some human. They didn't know what I was or what he'd done. Him holding my hand was a statement, and obviously, I hadn't the chance to talk to Tanner or Faye or Kalen. They would be so confused.

But I placed my hand in his, and my heart did a back handspring when he curled his fingers around mine, squeezing.

"You guys are so adorable," Tink said, tugging the hair I'd thrown up into a messy bun.

"You are," Caden said. "Especially when you blush."

"I'm not blushing." I watched Tink walk ahead, his long-legged pace taking him around the corner of the hall.

"Your face is the shade of a rose," he told me.

"It is not." I could feel my cheeks heat even more. "We need to focus on what's important."

"I am."

I glanced up at him and felt a little unsteady as my gaze met his. "Benji and finding out where they're getting the Devil's Breath is important."

"It is. But you're more important to me. You will always be the most important thing."

"You…" I swallowed, closing my eyes. "I wish we had time for me to tell and show you how perfect I think you are."

"I'm not perfect." He touched my cheek. "But I don't have a

problem with you showing me later how much you think I'm perfect."

Heat simmered in my veins. I planned on doing just that after I told him what needed to be shared.

But by the time we reached the end of the hall, I'd filed all of that away. What we were about to deal with needed our full attention.

The first person I saw when we turned the corner was Ren. Dressed in black, he leaned against the plain white wall, his back to us, ankles crossed. Tink was beside him. Fabian behind him, his blond hair draped over broad shoulders. He was the first to see us, his expression somber, and then there was a slight widening of his pale eyes.

Ren looked over his shoulder. "I was wondering when you were finally going..."

Either he trailed off, or I just didn't hear what he said because my gaze had been snagged by those remaining in the hall. Faye and Kalen stood with Tanner. There was an older male fae, as well, his silvery skin pale. He'd been pacing while Faye spoke to him quietly.

Maybe it was my imagination, but everyone seemed to stop and notice our joined hands. The message Caden was sending out had been received. We were together.

It was Kalen I zeroed in on because one side of his lips curved up a moment before he bowed slightly. "My King."

There was a flurry of the other fae beginning to do the same, but Caden stopped them with a slice of his hand through the air. "Is he in there?" He nodded at another nondescript door.

Stepping forward, Tanner cleared his throat. He looked shaken, and seeing Caden and I together had to be a part of it. He was likely seeing the crumbling of his entire Court, right in front of him. I wanted to tell him that it was okay, but now truly wasn't the time.

And time always seemed strange like that, because minutes kept ticking by, and they were never the right ones.

"Yes." Tanner sent a quick glance at me. "He's restrained."

"How is he?" Caden asked.

It was the man with Faye who spoke. "He is... He is not well." His voice cracked. "My King, he is not well at all."

Caden's hand slipped from mine as he stepped forward, placing his hand on the man's shoulder. "How is your wife, Balour?"

"Luce believes she will heal, but..." Balour looked away, lips pressed in a thin line. "I don't know who is in that room. He looks like my son. Sounds like him. But it is not Benji."

"I am sorry," Caden spoke, his voice low. "We will find who is responsible. They will pay."

"Thank you." The poor man struggled to take a breath as he looked at the closed door. "Is there any hope for him?"

"If there is, we will find it," Caden said. I hoped there was something to be optimistic about, but I doubted there was.

Tanner had inched closer, his voice low. "I...I didn't expect to see you here, Brighton."

"I didn't expect to be here either," I admitted, having no idea what else I could say other than, "We need to talk later."

"Yes, we do." He nodded, watching Caden as Benji's father turned, slowly walking away. My heart hurt for Balour.

Before I could respond to Tanner, Caden turned. "I want to speak with him."

"Of course." Tanner moved to open the door. "Do you want Kalen or Faye to join you? Or Prince Fabian?"

"Brighton will join me."

It took everything in me not to smile because doing so seemed wildly inappropriate given the circumstances.

Tanner looked as if he'd swallowed something that made him ill. "Of course."

"I would like to be a part of this," Faye said, lifting her chin. "He is my cousin."

Caden studied her for a moment and then nodded. Relief didn't flicker across her face. Steely determination lined her features.

Across from me, Ren pushed off the wall. "Be careful, he's a biter."

"Noted." Caden strode forward, stopping in front of me. "Ready?"

"I am."

"Okay." Then he lowered his head, and his lips met mine.

Caden kissed me, right there in front of everyone, hammering home the point that we were together.

The shock of Caden kissing me in front of everyone gave way to the all-too-brief burst of warmth and pleasure, of rightness.

He was mine.

And I was his.

Chapter 13

Benji was young.

He couldn't even be old enough to drink if he were human, and he looked so much like Faye. His hair was the same soft black, his skin a deeper, pewter shade, but those eyes were like Elliot's, the youngling Benji had gone in search of. They were pitch-black, so dark that the pupils weren't even visible.

The moment he saw the three of us, he pulled against the chains bolted to the wall. His hands were secured behind his back, and the length of the chain that connected to his ankles couldn't be more than a foot long, so he didn't make it very far.

He hissed though, the sound so eerily feline that the tiny hairs all along my body rose. His attention was focused on Caden.

"Hello, Benji," Caden said.

The youngling growled, his lips peeling back. "You're going to die."

"Is that so?" Caden replied flatly.

"You're all going to die." Benji looked at Faye and then to where I stood. He sniffed the air. "Especially you, human."

I rolled my eyes but remained quiet. This wasn't my interrogation. Although Caden hadn't said that, I knew I was here to listen. Not to engage. I wouldn't get anything out of Benji.

"And yet you're the one chained to the wall," Caden pointed out.

"For now."

Caden chuckled, the sound dark and cold. My gaze darted to him. "Do you really think you can escape me? Your King?"

Benji snapped at the air. "You're no longer my King."

"So, who do you answer to?"

"The one who gave us this world to rule, who will return humans to their rightful place as cattle," he snarled. "I answer to Queen Morgana."

Faye sucked in a sharp breath, her eyes squeezing shut.

"How can you answer to someone you've never met?"

"She will rip out your entrails and feast upon them."

"Sounds delightful, but you didn't answer my question, and my patience is already running thin."

Benji threw his head back, letting out a high-pitched whining sound. Jerking forward like a cobra striking, he snapped at the air again. "It doesn't matter if I've seen her. She will be freed, and you will bow to her. You will serve her."

"Thought she was going to rip out your entrails," I muttered.

Caden snorted.

Benji's head snapped in my direction. "She'll flay the skin from your bones, you stupid, fucking cattle. She'll—"

Benji's threats ended in a choking sound as Caden shot forward, clamping his hand down on the youngling's throat. "My patience ended right there. Look at me," he commanded. "Look at me, Benji."

Goosebumps pimpled my skin at the change in Caden's tone. It had lowered, but at the same time, seemed to blanket the room in soft, warm silk. I recognized the power in his words.

Glamour.

He was using glamour on another fae, something only the most powerful Ancients could do. And now I knew why he hadn't wanted me to be here. He'd been worried that seeing him use glamour to compel Benji to speak would remind me of Aric.

It was unnerving to be reminded of how powerful Caden was, but nothing about him made me think of Aric.

Benji quieted, his mouth hanging open as he stared up at Caden.

"Who do you answer to other than Queen Morgana?" Caden asked.

"I...I answer to the Winter Court," he answered numbly.

Faye opened her mouth as if she wanted to speak. I reached over, touching her arm slightly. She exhaled roughly and then nodded.

"Why do you answer to them?"

"Because they are..."

"They are what, Benji?"

"They are my masters."

Caden's head tilted slightly. He asked the question again, and then phrased the same question in a different way, but Benji, even under glamour, couldn't say why he answered to them.

And it became clear that several months of the boy's young life were simply *gone*. He couldn't say when he'd been here last. When he last drank any liquor. All he could repeat was that he answered to Queen Morgana, that he served the Winter Court, and that he only knew one name.

"Who is the Ancient who represents the Winter Court."

"Neal," he said. "I answer to Neal."

* * * *

After we left, Benji returned to his former state of hissing, snapping at the air, and threatening to kill everyone. We'd moved to one of the many meeting rooms on the first floor. Kalen and Faye sat beside Fabian, who was seated at one end of the table. Tink had moved off to the common area, where he could receive his daily dose of unfettered admiration. The fae loved him something fierce and were almost always in a constant state of awe around him, partly due to the fact that many had never seen a brownie. Ren was beside me, and Ivy was supposed to head over once she was done with her meeting with Miles. Fabian sat to my left at the other end of the table, and beside him, across from me, was Tanner. Where everyone was seated seemed to be important because when Caden pulled out my chair, every fae in the room stared as if he'd kissed me in front of them once more.

"Even under glamour, Benji couldn't answer why he serves the Winter Court," Caden told the room. "He doesn't know, not on an conscious or subconscious level."

"He has no memory. It's like his life has simply been wiped away," I said. "The only thing I've seen like that is a few humans who've been fed on and under glamour for long periods, but still, never to this level."

"I haven't seen it either," Ren agreed. "Could it be the Devil's Breath then?"

"It would have to be," Fabian answered. "I cannot think of anything that would strip the will and thoughts so deeply."

"They basically become a minion of the Winter Court without reason." Ren dragged his hand through his hair. "This isn't good."

That was the understatement of the year.

I looked over at Caden. "He knew Neal's name, though. That was the only other name he could say."

Caden nodded. "That doesn't tell us if Neal is still in the city or active. I couldn't get anything else out of Benji."

"And we already knew that Neal was involved and have checked out his bar. There was no sign of the Devil's Breath there," Fabian stated, his fingers tapping on the table.

"We need to find Neal," I said, thinking more in terms of how I would do it if this were something the Order was handling. "He has to be the key here."

"We've been searching the city, as has the Order," Tanner said, nodding at Ren. "If he's still here, he's gone to ground. But with Aric's death, I'm willing to bet he's left the city."

"It's not like there aren't places he can hide that we haven't looked or thought to check," Ren pointed out. "And given how many Winter fae are here, he'd have a lot of help doing so."

"I'm in need of refreshments." Tanner rose. "What would everyone like?"

Ren and Caden asked for water. Fabian and Kalen had gone for a soda, and my tongue tingled at the thought of carbonated goodness. I knew one soda wouldn't harm the baby, so I requested one too.

Tanner nodded. "Faye, why don't you help me?"

She blinked as if coming out of a daze and rose. I nibbled on my lip, watching her follow Tanner out. I wasn't the only one whose eyes were glued to her. Kalen had been like a hawk where she was concerned, his gaze flickering to her every few seconds.

"Do you think she'll be okay?" I asked when the door closed behind them.

"They were close, more like siblings than cousins." Kalen tipped his head back. "She'll be okay. Eventually."

Eventually always sounded manageable, except it could be a lifetime from now.

"So you think there's no hope for this kid?" Fabian asked.

"All of the others who consumed Devil's Breath had to be…put down," Caden said, his elbow propped on the arm of the chair as he dragged his thumb along his lower lip. "I imagine if Benji hadn't been restrained, the same would've happened to him."

"But we have one alive," I said. "That means we can at least find out if this is reversible. Hopefully, in the process, we can figure out how the Devil's Breath is able to make these younglings loyal to the Queen—a person they've never met."

Ren kicked back in his chair, planting a boot on the table. "The *borrachero* drug can make humans compliant, but that's only for a short period of time and when they're under the influence."

"Hopefully the specimens Luce took from Benji will tell us if he's still under the influence." Fabian crossed his arms. "If not..."

"Then there is no option," Caden said. "He will have to be given peace."

His brother nodded.

"He can't be kept here where there's a threat of him escaping, causing more harm." Kalen dropped his hand on the table. "His family will understand that."

"Will they?" I asked. "Truly?"

Kalen's gaze met mine. "No one here will ever risk the whole of the Court for just one. Not even for their family."

That seemed harsh, but I fully understood it.

"Except there is someone here who isn't just willing to risk the Court," Caden said, his thumb stilling under his lip. "But who is actively working against the Court."

"You think whoever that is has something to do with Benji coming home?" Ren asked.

"The youngling didn't indicate as much, but it would be unlikely that they aren't connected," Caden answered.

"So that leaves the question of what the goal of having Benji come back here was," Ren asked. "To cause mayhem? Remind the Summer Court that even though Aric is dead, the Winter Court is still very much active?"

My stomach dipped a little at the mention of Aric.

"Or Benji was acting as a scout. Or at the very least, a test," Fabian said, his gaze meeting his brother's from across the table. "He could've been sent here to see what was going on, in the hopes he'd get back out."

Caden's jaw tightened.

"Or he was sent as a test against our defense systems." Kalen nodded slowly. "But that doesn't seem as likely. Why wouldn't whoever the Summer fae is that's working with them be able to give them that information?"

I thought about the Order, how there was a hierarchy involved. There was one here, as well. "Maybe the fae helping the Winter Court isn't privy to the kind of information that could tell them how weak or strong your defenses are." Several gazes landed on me. Still unused to speaking up, I found being the center of attention unnerving. "It doesn't have to be someone any of us know. It could literally be any fae. And to me, it makes more sense that Benji was a test instead of a scout. If the Winter Court truly has no idea how prepared Hotel Good Fae is or not, they can't be stupid enough to only expect Benji to make it back."

Ren's lips pursed as he nodded.

"You have a point." Respect flashed in Caden's eyes as he looked at me. "A test does seem more likely."

"Not that any of this isn't important," Ren said, and Caden arched a brow. "But Benji was all hail Queen Morgana, talking like her coming back wasn't something in the distant future but more like an event not too far from now. Was that crazy talk, the dying battle cry of the Winter Court? Or something we need to be concerned about?"

The door opened then. Tanner returned with Faye. Luce was behind them, carrying the bottles of soda under her arm and a file in her other hand. She saw me and did a double-take.

I slid a little in my seat. Yet another person I needed to talk to STAT.

Tanner told Luce who had the sodas in a low voice. She placed one in front of me, her eyebrow raised. I gave her a sheepish grin.

"The Winter Court is nowhere near uttering their final, dying battle cry. Unfortunately," Caden said, nodding his thanks to Tanner as he placed a glass of water in front of him, "even without some of the Ancients, they are so very much a threat, but the doorways to the Otherworld are sealed. They cannot be reopened."

My gaze flicked to Tanner as he sat across from me. The doors could be reopened, but as much as I liked Ren, I would not trust him with that information. I wouldn't trust any Order member with that.

A shock surged through my system. I wouldn't trust any Order member? Wasn't I one? Could I even still be one once married to the freaking King of the Summer fae? Sure, they'd kept Ivy on, and she was a halfling. And Miles was open to things that other sects would've been dead set against. But Caden had…well, Caden was different.

Did I even want to be an Order member?

Being part of the Order was ingrained in my blood and bones. What would I be without my duty? Not that there was anything wrong with being a wife and a mother, but I needed more than that.

But the better question was, should I even still be Order when I wouldn't turn over highly necessary information about how the gates could be opened at any time by Caden?

While I had my little moral crisis, Caden was saying, "Unless she's somehow tripled in power, which is impossible, there is no way for her to physically open the gate."

"They can worship her like she's a god," Fabian chimed in. "But they cannot free her simply by praying for it to happen. What they would need is impossible."

Not exactly…

I wasn't sure if Ren accepted the answer or not, but he quieted as I unscrewed the lid of the bottle. There was no fizz. Was it flat? I sighed, but flat soda was better than none. I took a drink, relieved to feel some carbonation, although it sort of tasted like…like diet? I checked the bottle just to make sure I could read properly. It wasn't diet. Looking up, I saw Fabian frowning at his opened bottle.

"Luce has some information to share," Tanner announced, drawing my attention.

Luce nodded. "I was able to do a rapid test thanks to Benji's affinity for spitting when I went in to see him."

My lip curled as I took another drink.

"I was also able to get a urine sample," she said, and Caden's brows lifted. "You do not want to know how I accomplished that."

"I was there for it. She is right," Ren tossed out.

"I'll take both of your words on that," Caden said, and I grinned a little.

"This isn't entirely comprehensive." She opened the folder. "But from his saliva, I was able to determine that he hadn't consumed any alcohol in the last two hours, but there were trace amounts in his urine."

"What does that mean?" Faye asked.

"It means that he drank at some point in the last ninety days, but not recently, and not a lot. If the Devil's Breath is still being mixed with nightshade and liquor, I don't believe he's consumed any of it in the last couple of days."

Faye started to speak and then stopped to swallow before finding her voice. "But we don't know how long the Devil's Breath influences a fae."

"From what I've learned about the *borrachero*, it's that it only stays in a human's system for four hours and then is utterly undetectable in blood tests," Luce stated carefully.

I recognized that tone. Not the greatest news was coming. I started to drown my sorrow in my soda.

"I can one hundred percent say that it works the same in one of us— that it's only effective in terms of making one susceptible to persuasion for a short period of time. But there were no traces of scopolamine—the drug most similar here—in his system." Luce drew in a shallow breath. "I know these results don't tell us much."

"But what do you think it does tell us?" Caden asked, sensing there was something she wanted to add.

"This isn't my specialty," she started.

"I know. Tell us what you think."

She nodded curtly as she folded her hands over the file. "I think that Devil's Breath is only a part of the equation here. We know certain drugs and food and drinks react differently in us. Nightshade for example is poisonous to humans, but it gives us the same effect as some alcoholic beverages do. We also know that scopolamine, in most forms, is absolutely harmless to humans and fae. It's a common ingredient in motion sickness medication but when it's chemically processed into what we know as Devil's Breath, it's a different story. The fae could obviously be susceptible to it, but I have no reason to believe that it wouldn't have worn off by now. Very few human drugs have any impact on us."

Faye shook her head. "What…what does that mean exactly?"

"What I believe that means is there is a missing link. Something we don't know," she said. "And I know that's not exactly helpful, but there has to be something used or done in addition to this drink. Finding out what that is may be the key to stopping this more long-term influence over us."

"That actually tells us something," Caden said. "More than we knew."

"You don't think he'll come out of this then, do you?" Faye asked.

"I…I don't want to say for sure, but…" She pressed her lips together and then exhaled roughly. "But he's been here long enough for the effects to have worn off, and with nothing showing in his samples, I don't believe it is something reversible without knowing what the missing link is."

Faye closed her eyes as my stomach churned sharply with sympathy.

"I'm not saying he has to be…handled immediately. He's contained," Luce said. "We could wait."

Caden looked to Tanner, who gave a quick nod. "We could."

"No. I mean no offense." Faye opened her eyes. "I know you're suggesting that to be kind. Both of you. But there's no point."

"We can wait," Kalen insisted in a low voice.

"I knew the moment I saw him, he was gone," Faye said. "I knew deep down. There is nothing left of Benji in him. He's already gone, and there is no reason for us to delay this. Doing so won't make this easier for anyone."

A muscle ticked in Caden's jaw. "I can do it whenever you and your family are ready."

My stomach twisted again as I thought of Caden having to be the one to do that. It might be his duty, but who would want that kind of responsibility? What had been done to Benji wasn't his fault. I shifted, uncomfortable.

"I would." Faye's voice steadied. "I would ask your permission to allow either me or another member of his family to carry this out. We are all yours, but—"

"But he belongs to you and yours. I understand," Caden said. "Let me know when you wish to do it. I would like to be there just in case you decide you would prefer that I handle it."

"Of course. I...I need to speak to his father and check in on his mother," she said.

"Go," Caden issued quietly. "I'll await word."

Faye slipped quietly from the room, Kalen's eyes on her as he opened his soda.

"I'm sorry." Luce sat back, hands falling to her lap. "I wish I had more information. Something better than there being a missing link."

"Like I said, that is more than we knew before," Caden told her.

"He's right," Ren agreed. I think it was Ren. Or maybe it was Fabian. I wasn't sure.

I felt...weird.

Like not in a weird headspace, but like I had a few years ago when I'd been out to dinner with my mom. It had been a good night. She'd been herself, and we'd gone to one of her favorite seafood places. The shrimp had gone bad or something. Within an hour of eating, I'd quarantined myself in the bathroom. That was how I felt now.

But I hadn't eaten anything since breakfast, and I didn't feel like I needed to use the bathroom. Sweat dotted my forehead.

"Is it just me," I heard Kalen say, maybe to Fabian, "or does this soda taste weird?"

A sharp cramp sliced through my stomach, forcing me to lean back in my seat. Another knifing pain hit my midsection. It felt like period cramps but on steroids.

"Brighton?" Caden turned to me. "Are you okay?"

"Yep," I forced out, breathing through the rippling pain. "I just…"

Across from me, Tanner frowned. "You don't look well, Brighton."

I didn't feel well. Mouth strangely dry, I reached for the soda.

Caden started to rise, but it was Kalen who shot to his feet, his bottle in hand. "Don't touch that!" he yelled. "Don't take another drink."

Chapter 14

Startled, I drew my hand back. "W-what?"

"What's going on?" Caden demanded.

"The soda doesn't taste right," Kalen said, placing it on the table. "What does it taste like to you, Brighton?"

Heart jumping, I placed my damp hands against my stomach. There had to be a fist in there, clenching my insides. "I don't know. I thought it kind of tasted like diet."

"Like artificial sweetener?" Luce pushed from her seat, her pale eyes wide. "Maybe a little minty?"

"Yeah." I nodded as Caden knelt beside me. "I mean, I didn't taste mint, but…" But now that I thought about it, that could've been what I was tasting but couldn't place.

"Shit." Kalen gasped as Fabian picked up his bottle, sniffing it.

"What the hell is going on?" Ren asked as Luce hurried around the table.

"I second that question," Caden said. "And I want to know what the fuck is happening."

Luce slipped into the space between Ren's and my chairs. "Are you feeling sick?" She placed her hand against my forehead. "Nauseous? Cramps?"

"I…" I found it hard to swallow. "Yes."

Her features tightened and then smoothed out as she looked over at Caden. "I need you to get her to the infirmary."

"What…what is happening?" I whispered as Ren rose, giving us space.

Luce didn't answer. "Let me examine you—"

"I swear," Caden growled, "If I have to ask one more time what is going on, no one in this room is going to like it."

"I know you have questions, but right now, what's important is that we get her to a place where I can monitor her." Luce straightened, calm and collected as her gaze met mine. When she spoke next, there was a world of meaning in what she *didn't* say. "I need to examine you, Brighton. Privately."

Privately.

I looked at Caden, whose features had become stark. *Privately.* Understanding surfaced, and my heart kicked into overdrive.

The baby.

Panic sank its icy claws into me. I gripped the arms of the chair, and then it hit me—the strange sensation of wet warmth.

Standing abruptly, I pushed the chair back. Someone was speaking. It was Caden. His hand was on my arm, worry filling his golden eyes.

My stomach seized. There was no other warning. No stopping what came next. All I was able to do was turn away before my upper digestive system revolted. I doubled over, eyes and throat stinging as everything I'd consumed in the last day made a painful reappearance.

Caden was there, his hand on my shoulder. I tried to wave him away, but the clenching motion swept through me once more. I squeezed my eyes shut.

"I'm sorry—" I gagged.

"It's okay, sunshine." His voice sounded all wrong—panicked. "*Luce.*"

I opened my eyes and then tore my gaze away from the vomit. Staring at that wasn't going to help. But suddenly, I was in Caden's arms, and I was staring up at the ceiling. There were voices—shouts, and then I heard Caden.

"She's bleeding," he said, running his hand down my stomach and then around my back. "I don't know from where, but she's bleeding."

In a daze, I saw it. It was small, just a few smudges of red, right where I'd been sitting. I knew what it was even as my legs and arms seemed to no longer be attached to my body.

Blood.

There was blood on the chair.

How much blood did it take for it to soak through clothing? I knew where that sensation of wet warmth had come from—where the blood had come from.

The baby.

Another series of cramps seized me, and I twisted in Caden's arms, gagging. He lifted me off the floor. I must've checked out because the next thing I knew, I was being laid down on a thin mattress. Luce was at my side, my arm in her hand as another fae wrapped a blood pressure cuff around my biceps.

Caden's face was above mine, his hand warm against my cheek as he smoothed the hair back from my face. "It's okay," he said. "It's going to be okay. I promise you. Everything is going to be just fine."

But it wasn't.

You didn't bleed like that when you were pregnant. You didn't have pain like this. You didn't vomit like that.

Something was wrong—very wrong as the fae called out numbers that didn't sound right. There was a pinch in my arm. My head lolled to the side. Luce was inserting a needle. Dark red blood filled a collection tube.

"I need activated charcoal," Luce called out, rattling off milligrams and then fluids as hands lifted up my shirt. I jerked at the cool touch of ECG leads. There was beeping, and I thought it sounded too fast.

"Has she been poisoned?" Caden demanded, and it felt like the temperature of the room had increased. "Has someone poisoned her?"

"I'm not sure." Luce hooked up an IV as she looked over her shoulder. "But you should pull all the drinks you got from the cafeteria, Tanner."

"On it," came the quick reply from somewhere in the room.

Poisoned? Oh God. Panic overshadowed the deep contractions, giving way to terror as my gaze found Luce's. There was only one thought occupying my mind as I tried to drag in air, but the corners of my vision darkened. "Is the baby okay?"

Luce momentarily froze as she stared down at me.

"The baby?" Caden's voice was low, barely above a whisper. "*What* baby?"

Blinking rapidly, Luce's chin jerked up, and then her gaze shot back to mine. Her lips moved, but the beeping from the machines was rapid, and then darkness spread out. The room was suddenly shaking, the gurney creaking—

"She's having a seizure," Luce grabbed my shoulders. "No. Not the Ativan. I need—"

Whatever she said was lost in a roar and a burst of a hundred stars. The last thing I saw was Caden staring down at me in shock

And then I saw nothing.

* * * *

The first thing I became aware of was the steady beep of a machine. My head felt as if it were full of cotton balls so I focused on the sound and followed it out of the nothingness. It took a small eternity for me to open my eyes.

A light from somewhere behind me cast a soft, buttery-yellow glow over the room. I thought this was the same room I'd been brought into it, but it was…quieter. Calmer. On the small table was my iron cuff, blade disengaged.

The baby.

I moved my hand to my stomach, wincing at the pull of the IV. I had no idea what I was feeling for. The act seemed instinctual, but it told me nothing. Was the baby okay? My heart turned over heavily as fear hit my veins. It was strange how quickly I'd gone from being shocked and overwhelmed by the idea of having a baby, to desperately wanting that child.

Now it could be all over—gone before I even had a chance to share the news with Caden. And how could it have survived? I had a vague memory of Kalen yelling at me to not drink any more soda. Had I been poisoned? Grief and confusion swirled through me.

"Brighton."

Slowly, I turned my head to the left. Caden was sitting there, his chin propped on his joined hands. He looked…terrible. His normally smooth hair looked as if he'd dragged his fingers through the strands a hundred times. There were shadows under his eyes, and tension to the set of his lips. A wicked sense of deja vu hit me. It wasn't all that long ago that we'd found ourselves in a similar situation, but this time was different. The way he looked at me was…. It wasn't right.

"How are you feeling?" he asked.

My lips felt dry as I considered his question. My stomach didn't hurt, and I wasn't vomiting. "Okay." My voice was hoarse. "I think."

He reached over, picking up a pitcher and pouring a glass of water. "You should drink this."

I took the water, welcoming the cool rush against my scratchy throat. It helped clear some of the fog that seemed to still fill my brain. I would've drunk the entire cup if Caden hadn't caught the bottom of the glass, tugging it away.

"I think that's enough for right now." He placed the cup on the table.

"Luce warned that your stomach might be sensitive."

"What...what happened?"

"You were poisoned."

I tensed. *The baby.* "So hearing that said wasn't a figment of my imagination?"

"No." He sat forward, hands falling to the space between his knees. "It was done with a flower similar to Pennyroyal found in the Otherworld. Fae often use it as a powder for inflammation or bruises. We believe it was placed in the sodas."

I tried to process what he was saying. "All of them?"

He nodded. "The rest of the drinks have been pulled and are being tested, but the ones Fabian and Kalen had, also had traces of it."

"Are they okay?"

"They won't be affected by such a substance."

"Because they're fae?"

A muscle twitched in his jaw. "Because you're pregnant."

I drew in a shallow breath, but it went nowhere.

"The flower, when consumed in large quantities, can cause expectant mothers to miscarry," he continued, his voice strangely flat. "Luce believes it affected you more because you're mostly human, causing the vomiting and the seizure." He inhaled deeply. "And she believes that is also why you survived. Someone fully human wouldn't have. You'll be weak for a while. You may have more seizures, but she believes that you will recover fully."

It connected in the back of my mind that he must've told Luce about the Summer Kiss, but that didn't matter at the moment. His features blurred as tears filled my eyes. My brain wasn't working right. A part of me knew that this wasn't how I'd wanted Caden to find out. How I'd planned on any conversation about the baby going, but I had to know. Even though I was terrified, I had to know.

"Is the...am I still pregnant?" I whispered.

His eyes closed briefly. "The poison caused you to have contractions, which created a tear and then the bleeding. Luce was able to get the poison out of your system quickly."

I could feel myself trembling as I tried to brace for the inevitable.

"Once she had you stabilized, she was then able to check on the...on the baby." His throat worked on a swallow. "Luce didn't find any tissue in your bleeding. She did an ultrasound—sonography—to check for a heartbeat." He took a shuddering breath, his eyes meeting mine.

"According to Luce, the baby is incredibly strong-willed and determined to be born."

I blinked once and then twice. "W-what?"

"You didn't lose the baby. At least, not now," he explained. "She said it's a high-risk pregnancy and that you need to be monitored, but she's cautiously optimistic."

"I... I'm...." Stunned, I couldn't find words as disbelief rose. "I'm still pregnant?"

Caden nodded.

Tears welled so fast that I smacked my hands over my face. Relief and happiness turned out to be way more powerful than the crushing dread and fear. I couldn't believe it. This baby has survived Aric and a poisoning. Strong-willed was an understatement.

"Are those tears of happiness?" Caden asked. "Or disappointment?"

I yanked my hands away from my face. "What?"

"I think it's a valid question," he said. "Because I don't know if you're happy or sad to know that you're still pregnant."

"I'm happy," I told him, shocked. "Why would you even ask that?"

"Why?" A harsh, short laugh left him. "How would I know what you're thinking? You've known this whole time that you were pregnant. Eleven weeks, actually. Luce was able to confirm definitively, by the way."

I gave a little shake of my head. "I'm happy. I want this baby—"

"You do?"

"Yes," I said without hesitation. "I was planning to tell you. That's what I wanted to talk to you about later." The cloudy feeling in my head had completely disappeared. "I didn't tell you, because—"

"Because you were trying to save the world. Yeah, I know. Luce told me." The tension brackets increased around his mouth and then he rose, turned away.

"Caden—"

"I didn't know," he said, voice rough. "I thought I was hearing things when you asked about the baby." His voice cracked on that word, and I felt it in my heart. "I learned that I was going to be a father at the same time I learned that someone out there knew and tried to kill not only you but also my child."

"I was trying to do the right thing," I told him. "I was doing the right thing—"

"I stood there, trying to process that someone had almost killed you and my child," he cut me off. "And in the midst of watching you nearly die and being unable to do a damn thing, I realized that the only reason Kalen knew to tell you not to drink any more of that soda was because he knew that you were pregnant."

"I'm sorry. He wasn't supposed to know. He overheard me telling Tink—"

"I know." He faced me. "He knew. So did Tanner. So did Faye. Are there any more who are sworn to be loyal to me that knew you were carrying my child?"

"No. They weren't supposed to know. I told Tink because I had to tell someone—"

"You should've told *me*, Brighton."

"I wanted to. I did. But I thought that if you knew, it would be harder for us to do the right thing—"

"Doing the right thing never should've included you keeping the fact that you were pregnant with my child from me." His eyes weren't cool then. They burned with anger. "I get what you were trying to do. Your desire to protect my Court and others is something that I love about you, but this is different."

"How is it different?" I tried to sit up but found it was harder than expected. Caden snatched a pillow from the counter and shoved it behind my back. "Thank you."

"That is our child, Brighton. Not just yours. Ours." After ensuring that I was sitting up easily, he stepped back from the bed. "And *our* child should matter more than everything else. That's why it's different."

"I agree, Caden, that's why I needed you to choose a Queen because I didn't want our child to grow up in a world that was being overrun by Winter fae," I reasoned, trying to keep my voice calm.

"I chose you as my Queen."

"But I didn't know that!" The heart monitor beeped loudly, earning a dangerous look from Caden. I forced myself to calm down. "I didn't know, and I planned to tell you tonight—"

"You mean last night. You've been out for almost twelve hours."

"Oh," I whispered.

He shoved a hand through his hair again. "This isn't the time for this conversation. You need to take it easy—"

"I am taking it easy, and there is no other time we should be having this conversation. I'm sorry, Caden. You have to believe that. I wanted to tell you. If you don't believe me, you can ask Tink. You can even ask Tanner. I wanted—"

"Then why didn't you tell me the moment you realized we could be together?" he asked.

"I was just overcome. I knew I should have, but my head was all over the place," I admitted. "I thought we had time."

"You thought wrong," he said, and my gaze flew to his. "If I had known, I could've stopped what happened."

"How?" I asked. "How could you have stopped this? If someone wants me dead, whether or not I'm pregnant won't change that. You said this flower or whatever would've most likely killed me if I hadn't been given the Summer Kiss."

"If I had known, I would've made sure you weren't given something that could've killed our child."

"How? Are you going to taste everything I eat and drink?"

"Fuck, yes!" he shouted. "I would taste everything that wasn't prepared by my hands."

"And if I wasn't pregnant, you would've been like YOLO then? Let me drink whatever?"

His eyes narrowed. "It would've taken a lot more than that to kill you. And no, that doesn't mean I wasn't or wouldn't be worried about someone targeting you, but at least I know that you wouldn't be easy to kill. Our child is a whole different story."

I dragged my hand over my face, realizing then that he was a hundred percent serious about tasting my food and drink. "I...I don't know what to say other than I understand why you're upset. I do. And I hope you understand why I didn't say anything. But I'm sorry, Caden. I don't know what to say to make this better."

Jaw working, he looked away. "Neither do I."

My chest squeezed. "What...what does that mean?"

"I don't know. I really don't," he said, and my chest clenched. "If I hadn't told you that you being with me wouldn't be a risk, when were you going to tell me?"

"I planned on telling you as soon as you were married—"

"So, you were going to wait until I did what? Moved on from you? Picked a fae?" He took a step toward the bed. "Did you really believe that I would just choose to be with someone else when I knew that you love me? That I would've just walked away?"

"Before I knew that I could be with you, that's what I'd hoped you would do," I admitted. "I wouldn't have liked it. I would've hated it—loathed every second of it—but it was the right—"

"You can believe all you want that it was the right thing to do. Maybe on a superficial level, it was, but our child changes that. Keeping that knowledge from me was never the right thing. Not when you love me. Not when you know I love you." He turned, his body stiff. "And the worst part of this is the fact that you really believed I would move on. That I could just happily go and marry someone else."

"I didn't think you'd do that happily."

"But you told Tanner to do whatever was necessary to make sure I married a fae," he shot back, and I stiffened. "Yes, he told me how the woman I love conspired with others to make sure I ended up with someone else while she was carrying my child."

It felt like my heart had stopped. "I didn't conspire. It wasn't like that. I couldn't risk the whole world. Not when our child would have to grow up in it." My hand went to my stomach. "What I was trying to do doesn't change that I love you, Caden."

"But you didn't love me enough to fight for me, did you? You didn't love me enough to trust that things would be okay." His jaw hardened. "And you sure as fuck didn't respect me enough to tell me about our child."

"Caden—" I started, but the door opened then, revealing Luce. "Can you give us a moment?"

"I don't think so." Luce was rocking one hell of a no-nonsense tone and expression. "I've been monitoring Brighton's heart rate and blood pressure remotely, and I apologize, my King. I know you two have a lot to discuss, but we need to keep her heart rate and pressure stable."

"I'm fine."

"This is not keeping her stable," Luce continued as if I hadn't spoken. "And so soon after everything, this could threaten the pregnancy."

"You're right." Caden folded his arms. "When do you think it will be safe to move her?"

"I think tomorrow will be fine, as long as her stats remain stable, and she's kept as…" She glanced over at me. "Stress-free as possible."

"She will be," barked Caden, and I raised my brows. "I don't want her here for one second longer than necessary."

"Understood."

Caden turned to me. "When we leave tomorrow, you'll be coming home with me."

"To your apartment?"

"No. To a place very few are aware of," he said. "And do not argue with me about this and cause yourself unnecessary stress. Your house is not suitable."

Too much was happening, and strangely, my brain focused on that statement. "Why is it not suitable?"

"Because too many people know where to find you, and I cannot possibly begin to secure the house," he replied, turning back to Luce. "Notify me the moment you leave here."

She nodded.

There was no way he was leaving. "Where are you going?"

Caden didn't answer. He simply turned around and left the room, closing the door behind him without answering my question.

Without so much as looking at me.

Chapter 15

"He hates me."

"No, he doesn't." Tink patted my arm. He'd followed Luce in, advising that he was on the approved visitation list.

In other words, he was allowed to see me.

I had a feeling that Caden had prohibited everyone else from getting close to me, which was understandable. But Tanner and Faye? Kalen? Ren and Ivy? Fabian? They were the only ones I trusted, but apparently, Caden was taking no chances.

While that should give me some relief because it meant that he still cared, I had a sinking feeling that he was more worried about the baby.

After all, according to him, I wasn't all that easy to kill. Or whatever.

"You don't understand, Tink." I sighed as Luce came over to check my blood pressure. "He feels betrayed, and I can't blame him. Not really."

"Neither can I," he agreed. "But I think he just needs time. He knows you were trying to do the right thing."

I nodded.

"He was dealt one hell of a shock, learning he was a baby daddy while you were vomiting up your guts and seizing," Tink pointed out as bluntly as possible. "I imagine most expect to learn that kind of news in any other way than how the King learned it."

"I know. It's just…" I could still hear him saying that I hadn't loved him enough. That wasn't true. It was the exact opposite. I loved him enough to not be the source of his downfall, and I loved our child enough to do everything to bring him or her up in a world that was stable.

Well, as stable as it could be.

"Is everything still okay?" I asked as Luce placed the cuff on the counter.

"All of your stats look good." Luce came back to the bed. "I'll check the hormone levels in the blood I just took, and then I'll take some more blood tomorrow. If you were to start to miscarry, we'd see those hormone numbers going down."

My stomach dipped. "Do you think there's still a chance that I could lose the baby?"

"The pregnancy is considered threatened, so yes, there is a chance. But you're different, Brighton. You're not entirely human." Her pale eyes narrowed on me. "Which would've been something useful to know when I first examined you."

"Hey." Tink lifted his hands. "She didn't even tell me." He slid me a look. "Hussy."

I sighed once more. "I'm sorry. I didn't think it was something I was supposed to share, and in my defense, a whole lot of shit has been happening. I obviously haven't been making the best decisions."

"That's an understatement," Tink muttered under his breath as he leaned back in the chair.

I ignored that.

"Learning that you were given the Summer Kiss explains why you've been healing so well from your previous injuries," Luce went on. "Since you were given it before conception, it probably aided with that too. That's got to have something to do with the child being so resilient, but I can't be sure. I've never met a human who's been given the Summer Kiss." Her brow puckered. "But you stopped bleeding last night, so that's great news. You haven't been experiencing any more cramping or nausea, right?"

I nodded. "I feel normal-ish. My stomach is a little sore, and I feel like I just got over the flu or something."

She nodded. "That's normal. It appears your body is…well, repairing the damage. And to be honest, that is not something that would normally happen. Not even for a female fae who'd been given this poison."

Unease blossomed, but I tried to shut that down. Luce was giving me good news. Just because this was nothing short of a miracle didn't mean I'd lose the child.

"Luckily, we were able to get it out of your system as soon as possible. A few more minutes, I don't think even the Summer Kiss would've changed the outcome," she said, and that was hard to process. "I'm optimistic, but a lot is going to depend on what happens in the next couple of days to weeks."

"What can I do to make sure the baby is okay?"

Luce took a moment and then softened her voice. "In most of these circumstances, there is nothing you can do to change the outcome. It's often out of your hands. If you were to lose this child, it would not be your fault."

"I know, but there's got to be something I can do, right?"

"There are things that can help. One of them is to remain as stress-free as possible, and I know that is going to be hard, but keeping stress levels low is what you need to do," she advised, and I almost laughed, because I had no idea how I would do that. "I do suggest bed rest for the next week just to be safe."

Bed rest? "What about our appointment?"

"I think we can delay it a week since I've done a lot of the tests that I would've been doing, but I will be checking in on you—tracking your hormone levels." She folded her arms. "I would refrain from any physical activity until you feel completely one hundred percent—no longer sore or tired. That could be a week or slightly longer. No physical activities also includes sex."

I didn't think that would be an issue.

"You're going to need to keep your hands and body parts to yourself," Tink advised.

"Thanks for the clarification," I said. "I can do that. Bed rest and no physical activity. I'll do whatever I can to keep the baby healthy."

"That's good to hear," she said. "It's good that you'll be staying with Caden in a secure location."

"Because once the fae who tried to kill me realizes they failed, they'll come at me again?" Anger flashed through me, so potent and hot that Luce frowned at the color that highlighted my cheeks. "I can't believe someone tried that. I mean, I can, but what in the hell did they think they'd gain from killing me? That Caden would somehow revert back to his evil self and open the doorway? That's not how that works."

A huge part of me couldn't believe how easy I'd made it for them. I almost always drank soda when I was here. Any number of fae could've paid attention to that. I really needed to change up my routine.

"Perhaps they thought that by killing you, it would simply distract and weaken him. Which it would," Luce advised. "It could have nothing to do with their attempts to free their Queen, but more so to level a blow that our King would find difficult to recover from. Choosing a poison that affects pregnancy so adversely was extremely lucky for them—and most unfortunate for you."

I tried not to be offended by her word choice. "Do we have any idea who could've done it? Were the other bottles contaminated? Any other drinks?"

"So far, only about a dozen tested positive," she said.

"Are any of the fae here at risk?"

"We've notified those who are pregnant, and it doesn't appear that any have been put at risk," she answered.

"That's good news," I whispered, hands curling into the thin blanket.

"Caden has been holding an inquisition, questioning all the fae who had access to the drinks that were in the cooler," Tink said. "Which is pretty much every fae here."

It almost seemed like an impossible task, but Caden could compel the truth. Something that I doubted he wanted to do to every member of his Court without due cause. He was smart enough to know that he'd create more enemies using glamour to find the one who was responsible, but now he had a reason.

I just hoped it didn't hurt his relationship with his Court.

But I wanted whoever was responsible dead. Actually, I wanted to be the one to kill them myself. That would probably violate the whole bed rest thing, but I also thought it could be fairly therapeutic.

"You know, I've been thinking," Tink said. "And I know that usually means I'm about to say something completely irrelevant, but I promise that's not the case right now."

My brows rose. "What have you been thinking about?"

"Why do we think it's someone who didn't know you were pregnant?" Tink asked as he glanced between the two of us. "Because there are a lot of ways they could have tried to kill you—well, poison is definitely a quieter way, but there are other poisons they could have used. Right, Luce?"

"Right," she replied, drawing out the word.

"All I'm saying is that it seems way too coincidental that the poison that was chosen, was the one that has that kind of effect on a pregnancy."

A trickle of unease skirted through me. "But there are only a handful of people who know I'm pregnant. None of them would've done something like this."

"I don't think they would've, but that doesn't mean they didn't say something," Tink reasoned. "That everyone kept their mouth shut."

"You're suggesting that one of us jeopardized her safety?" Luce demanded. "I can tell you that those who know never would've done that."

"I'm not suggesting that anyone did it thinking it would jeopardize her safety," Tink responded. "Look, everyone talks. Even the fae. You may be special, Luce, and you're a fortress of secrets, but there ain't a single race of beings out there that isn't infected with the need to gossip."

"I get what you're saying, but those who know would never be so careless with such information."

"Maybe not." Tink sat back. "Perhaps they weren't so careless at all."

My gaze sharpened on him, but I didn't say anything until Luce finished up and left the room. "What are you really thinking? And don't say nothing. You were being purposely vague. Maybe Luce didn't see that, but I did."

Tink glanced at the door. "Okay. I was being a little vague, but Lite Bright, something doesn't seem right about this."

"A lot of things don't seem right at the moment."

"Yeah, but I just think it's strange that out of all the poisons—and there are many that have been brought over from the Otherworld—that would've killed you with just one taste, *that* one was used." His gaze slid back to me. "Sure, you were given a large dose that would've taken you out if you were completely human, but why take that risk when there are far more effective ones? Think *Game of Thrones* level of quick and messy death. It's almost like killing you wasn't the priority."

"If I wasn't the priority, then—" That was something I didn't want to even think. Because it would mean that the baby was the target, and that meant Tink was right. "Who would you think would've talked?"

"I don't know. I want to say none of them, but…"

"But you just said everyone gossips." There was a great sense of dread. "And you said maybe they didn't speak carelessly. I'm thinking you meant someone shared the news with intent."

"But I do agree that none of those who knew would've done anything to harm you. Kalen stopped you from drinking. Tanner wouldn't do something like that. He's too dignified. And what reason would Faye have?"

"And Luce?"

"She's had plenty of opportunities to end you or the baby."

True. She could've poisoned the prenatal pills, and no one would have known. "Then who could it have been?"

"Do we know that no one else was in the courtyard? No. We don't. Someone else could've been out there," he said. "Whatever fae is working with the Winter Court could've followed you, or it could be someone else."

"Then that would mean we have not one but two fae we need to locate."

Tink nodded. "And that Caden is definitely going to kill."

"Caden?" I coughed out a humorless laugh. "I'm going to kill the sons of bitches."

Chapter 16

After Luce had returned later with a light dinner, she wanted me to get up and move around a little, which consisted of me walking around the small room.

Then came the part I usually dreaded whenever I went to the doctor. She weighed me, and for once, seeing that I'd gained a few pounds even though I'd been a volcano of vomit the night before made me breathe a sigh of relief. She took some more blood, and after my twentieth or so lap around the room, I returned to the bed, surprised by how much that had worn me out.

"Like I said, you're going to be weaker than usual," she told me, slipping the vial of blood into a small bag. "But I have a feeling you'll regain your strength quicker than even I expect."

"The Summer Kiss, huh?" I leaned back against the mountain of pillows.

"It's a kiss of life." Luce placed the bag on the counter and then crossed her arms. Her gaze fell to the small table. I'd engaged the blade earlier, just in case. It was only a few inches in length, but it was long and sharp enough to do its job. "I wish you would've told me about that, and yes, I know I already said that, but I feel the need to restate it. I could've told you then that you had nothing to worry about when it came to our King choosing you—that *I* had nothing to worry about."

"I'm sorry. I didn't know that changed things. Caden never told me," I explained. "And I get why he didn't. He was trying not to overwhelm me after everything, but I wish he'd told me."

"And I'm sure he wished you'd told him about the child," she replied, and I flinched. "I meant no offense by that. What I mean is that it seems like you and Caden could've benefited from a very in-depth conversation."

I laughed dryly. "No doubt."

"But you have both been processing a lot," she said, picking up the bag.

"Have you seen Caden?" He hadn't been back.

"I believe he's still carrying out the questioning," she answered.

I wondered who was standing guard outside because I doubted Caden was relying on a locked door. But who had Caden deemed trustworthy enough? I picked at the blanket. "Who's playing babysitter?"

She arched a brow. "Kalen."

A slight smile tugged at my lips. "I owe him a lot. If he hadn't…"

Luce inclined her chin. "He would make a fine Knight for our King."

As far as I knew, Caden hadn't chosen any of his Knights yet. I had a feeling Aric's betrayal all those years ago played a role in that. "He would. I'm glad to see that Caden trusts him." I watched Luce slip the vial into her pocket, thinking about what Tink had said. I actually hadn't really stopped thinking about it. "Can I ask you something?"

She nodded. "Of course."

"Do you really think the choice of poison had nothing to do with my pregnancy? That it's possible that no one who knows spoke?"

"I've thought about this. It's an herb that's widely available—actually grown in our greenhouse as it has amazing healing properties. Some of the other poisons that Tink mentioned are simply not easily accessible. That could be the reason." She smoothed the lapel of her coat. "But if Tink is right, that one of those who knows did speak, who would they have told that would've done something like this? Would it then be a coincidence that the person unknowingly told the fae who has been working with the Winter Court, and if not, then are we dealing with two fae who have done the unforgivable?"

I nibbled on my lower lip, mulling it over. I couldn't shake the feeling that I was missing something. "Maybe this has nothing to do with the other fae. I mean, I'm sure there are tons of fae who would probably act upon the knowledge that I was pregnant."

"You don't seem to have a high opinion of the fae," she replied, "if you think there are so many who would wish to harm an unborn child. If you're to be our Queen, I hope that changes."

Chastised, I realized that what I'd said hadn't come out right. "I didn't mean that I think there's a ton of fae who would gladly harm a child, but I bet there are many who would do anything to protect their Court, right? Isn't that what Kalen said about Benji's family? That they wouldn't even keep their own child alive if it was a risk to the Court?"

Luce's brows puckered. "Yes. Many fae are willing to protect their Court," she said slowly.

"And how many fae would see me as a risk to the Court? Even before the pregnancy. After all, Tatiana came to me before I knew I was pregnant," I reasoned. "Without them knowing I'd been given the Summer Kiss, wouldn't they see this child as a threat to their future? It's why I hadn't told Caden that I was pregnant. It's why you agreed to remain silent, as did the others."

"I see what you're saying." She sighed wearily. "It's just that I have a hard time believing that those who knew would've said anything. That knowledge in the wrong hands doesn't only mean someone viewing you as a threat, but it could also cause panic."

"Then...then that person may have told someone they trusted. Someone who may have..." Someone who may not have been sent into a panic. Who would've already known that Caden was in love with me. Suspicion dawned, and I was grateful that I wasn't hooked up to the heart monitor.

"What?" Luce asked.

I didn't want to say anything in case I was wrong. "Can you do me a favor? Can you get Tanner for me?"

"Why do you want to see him?"

"I just thought of something he said to me, and I'm not sure if I heard him right," I lied. "Please? Tanner cannot possibly be banned from seeing me."

"The King decreed that no one without his express approval—"

"Or I can just go find Tanner myself. I doubt you're going to chain me to my bed. So, do you think Caden would be more upset with me roaming around, or you getting Tanner for me?"

Her eyes narrowed. "That sounds like blackmail."

"More like presenting you with options," I suggested.

One side of her lips curved up. "Uh-huh. I doubt you'll have any problems assuming the role of our Queen." She turned away. "I'll go find Tanner now."

"Thank you," I said, unsure if her comment about the whole Queen thing was a compliment or not.

But I didn't have the brain space to really deal with that. If my suspicions were on point, then I might know who poisoned the drinks.

When a soft knock came about fifteen minutes later, I knew Luce had done what I asked. Tanner stepped in, quietly closing the door behind him.

"Luce said you needed to speak with me?" he asked.

I nodded. "Thank you for coming, even though I have a feeling that Caden has told everyone to stay away from me."

A faint smile appeared. "He has, but Luce said that she sensed it was important." Walking forward, he sat in the chair. He looked rough, as if he hadn't slept well. Whether or not my suspicion was correct, he had to have a lot on his mind. "Luce told us that the child is well, which I'm grateful to hear. But how are you feeling?"

"I'm okay. Just a little tired. Thank you for asking."

The shadows under his eyes looked like bruises as he nodded. "I don't mean to be rude, but I'm confident that Kalen didn't even want to allow me into the room. I imagine the only reason I was allowed is because the King is with Faye and her family."

Benji.

Jesus, I'd practically forgotten about him. "He hasn't gotten better, has he?"

Tanner shook his head sadly. "He is…he is lost to us."

Sadness found its way into my already crowded heart. "They'll…" What had Caden said? Peace. "They'll give him peace now?"

He nodded. "Yes. Our King is there in case they have need of him."

I glanced at the door, wanting to go and find where they were. I wanted to be there for Caden, even if he didn't have to be the one to end Benji's young life. That suddenly seemed as important as why I'd asked for Tanner.

"I wouldn't want to further displease the King," Tanner said. "What did you want to see me about?"

"Understood." I drew in a shallow breath, fighting the urge to run off and find Caden. While I'd threatened to do that earlier, even I wasn't that stupid when there was someone out there actively trying to harm the baby and me. "I want to ask you something, and I hope you'll be honest. It's an uncomfortable question."

Tanner nodded for me to continue.

"Did you tell anyone that I was pregnant?" I asked, watching him closely. A muscle twitched near his right eye. "And I'm not suggesting that I think you told someone thinking they'd do what they did, but I know I told you to do whatever was necessary to make sure Caden chose a fae as his Queen, and I don't think you would've told just anyone because of the panic or risk it could cause. I know you would do anything to protect your Court, and maybe that included telling someone that I was pregnant. Maybe so they'd pursue Caden, knowing that Caden would eventually find out that I was pregnant."

Tanner stared at me in silence for several heartbeats. "You think I spoke to Tatiana?"

I nodded. That's exactly what I suspected—that he'd told Tatiana, maybe even her brother. "It would make sense. Tatiana and Sterling already knew what was happening in terms of the engagement. They would have a reason to view the child as a real threat. I don't want to believe it," I quickly added as Tanner's eyes widened. "I honestly think that Tatiana came to me in the beginning out of concern and not to get me to leave Caden. So, I'm not saying this out of jealousy or anything like that. Caden loves me." Even if he wasn't quite sure about that now. That thought hurt, but my suspicion wasn't coming from making the other woman who wasn't even really the other woman the villain. "It just makes sense."

Tanner leaned forward. "Tatiana would never do such a thing. Neither would her brother. I know you don't know them well, and I can even understand why you'd think it was them, but those misdeeds cannot be placed on them."

"Are you sure? How well do you know them?" I asked.

"I don't know either extremely well." Lifting a hand, he dragged it over his head, clasping the back of his neck. "But I know they had nothing to do with this tragedy."

Tragedy? As if what had happened was due to an unexpected car accident. "You mean attempted murder?"

His silvery skin paled as he tipped back, recoiling from what I'd said. A moment passed. "You're right. It was attempted murder. I..." He dropped his hand to the arm of the chair. "Caden gave you the Summer Kiss. He did this years ago?"

Caught off guard by the change of topic, it took me a moment. "Yes. When I was injured by Aric and the other fae. It was why I didn't die then."

"You are his *mortuus*," he said, his voice thickening as his gaze roamed over my face. "You hold a piece of his soul. That makes you a far more worthy choice than any fae that could be presented to him. The entire Court, once they are aware, will not only support his choice but will celebrate such a union. It is rare for one to find their *mortuus*."

"That's what Caden told me." Emotion clogged my throat, and I couldn't think about how things were now. "I didn't know what it meant until yesterday. He hadn't wanted to overwhelm me. If I knew, I never would've tried to hide my pregnancy from him, and I wouldn't have asked you to do that or to help make sure he chose someone else."

"I know." A small, sad smile appeared as his eyes glistened. "I wish he had told you. I wish I had paid attention enough to realize what you meant to him. Looking back, it was obvious. I should have known. I found my *mortuus* once, but I lost her."

"I'm sorry," I told him.

"It wasn't Tatiana or her brother." A tear slid unchecked down his cheek. "It was me."

Chapter 17

"I can barely live with myself now," Tanner said. "I can't let someone else take the blame for my actions. Not when this reckoning was always coming."

Blood pounded in my ears as I stared at Tanner in disbelief.

"When I saw him with you, I thought you'd changed your mind. That he'd convinced you to stay with him," he explained, staring at his open hands. "And I believed that after everything I'd done, the dirt I'd sunk my hands into, that it was all for nothing. That our King was going to forsake our entire Court."

I couldn't think.

"I didn't know if you'd already told him about the baby. I thought you hadn't, because if you had, I couldn't imagine that he'd allow you into the room with that poor youngling," he continued. "I thought that if I could at least end the pregnancy, it would cut one of the threads that bound him to you, and you to him. After all, it would not be the worst sin I have committed to protect the Court."

I couldn't move.

"In the beginning, I thought you were just a passing fancy and then a distraction. I knew he cared for you. Deeply enough that even if I hadn't known you were his *mortuus*, I saw that he would not easily choose another." His voice rasped, barely audible. "Aric lied to you, Brighton. There was no Summer fae willing to work with the Winter Court to release that monster. There was only me."

I couldn't breathe.

"I knew I could get a message to him through Neal, and I did. I met with him twice, and there was a moment when I considered killing him.

I'd brought a sheathed dagger with me. I could've done it. The Ancient was so arrogant. I had a window of opportunity." He continued staring at his hands. "But I didn't take it. Not the first time when I told him that...that you were important to our King, and not the second when he told me that he planned to use you to force Caden to open the gateway. I didn't know then that was possible. I thought..."

The shock of what he'd admitted snapped me out of my stupor. "You...*you're* the reason Aric came for me? You knew that he had me alive? That he was keeping me there, torturing—?"

"I thought he would kill you. I didn't know he'd keep you alive," he said without looking up.

"You thought...he would kill me. As if that makes a difference, makes it better," I whispered, disbelieving what I was hearing.

This was Tanner.

Prim and proper Tanner, who wore polo shirts and khaki pants. Who I could easily imagine playing golf on the weekends. Tanner, who was nice and always calm, who I knew had harbored a crush for my mother and had been genuinely upset over her murder.

Murder carried out by the Ancient he'd later all but handed me over to.

And now he'd tried to kill my child.

"How could you?" I demanded, hands shaking. The betrayal cut so deeply that it was all I could feel. It hurt, because never in a million years would I have expected that he'd do something like this. It *hurt*.

"It wasn't personal."

"Are you serious?" I cried. "How could this get any more personal?"

"I know that sounds absurd. I like you, and you know I liked your mother—"

"How could you do this? I trusted you. My mom trusted you." A rising tide of anger chipped away at the pain of his betrayal. "Caden trusted you."

"I know." He lifted his head then. Tears tracked down his face, and seeing them made me even more furious. What right did he have to be upset? He'd tried to kill our child. He was responsible for my seemingly never-ending weeks in hell. "I thought I was doing the right thing." He sat back, arms limp at his sides. "Caden thought he was doing the right thing by not telling you everything. You thought you were doing the right thing by pushing him away and not telling him about the baby. And I thought I was—"

"What you did is not even remotely the same," I snapped. "We were trying to protect one another. You—"

"And I was trying to protect the entire Court and the world!" His shoulders shook. "That's what I was trying to do."

I stared at him, trembling. The rage building inside of me diminished everything else—the betrayal, the disbelief, and the pain. I'd told Tink that I would kill whoever had been responsible. I wasn't being overdramatic then, and that was before I knew that the person responsible for nearly ending my child's life was also responsible for the horror I'd suffered at Aric's hands. Out of the corner of my eye, I saw the cuff and blade on the table.

Murderous fury was a cyclone inside of me. I liked Tanner. I trusted him. My mom had trusted him, and maybe later, the pain of his betrayal would haunt me, but the bitter burn of vengeance consumed me now. I moved without thinking, twisting at the waist as I kicked the blanket off. I reached for the cuff, fully intending to slam the blade deep into his throat. I would sever his head from his shoulders, ensuring his death.

Tanner was quick, like all fae were, no matter if they fed or not.

He shot from his chair, knocking it over as he swiped up the cuff with a linen napkin that had been left beside it.

Shit.

Sliding off the bed, I grabbed the lamp just as the door burst open. I yanked the lamp from where it was plugged in and swung it at Tanner as Kalen burst into the room.

"What the hell is going on?" Kalen demanded as Tanner jumped back, blocking the blow with his other arm. The ceramic base shattered, cutting into his flesh. "Brighton!"

"It's him!" I shouted, refusing to take my eyes off Tanner. "He poisoned me. He handed me over to Aric!"

"What?" Disbelief filled Kalen's voice.

"It's true." Tanner backed up, his gaze briefly darting to where Kalen stood inside the room. "She speaks the truth."

"What?" Kalen repeated, denial still evident in his tone.

"I was trying to protect the Court." Tanner kept backing up.

"I don't care what you were trying to do!" I screamed. "We trusted you!"

"Tanner." Horror had replaced the shock in Kalen's voice. "Our King will kill you."

"No, he won't," I said, hands balling into fists. "Because I'm going to kill him first." I took a step forward.

"That won't be necessary." Tanner's back hit the wall as his tear-stricken pale gaze met mine. "Neal has left the city. I know you have no reason to believe me, but I have nothing to gain by lying. Neal is gone." The thin linen wasn't giving much protection against the iron. Wisps of smoke drifted from the cloth and the fae's skin. "Aric didn't tell me you were the King's *mortuus*, but he would've told Neal. He may be gone, but he knows you're the King's greatest weakness. And he would've told others. They'll come for you, thinking they can use you to control the King. Do what I failed to do. Protect the King and the future of my Court. Never let your guard down."

It happened so fast.

Tanner jerked his hand back, then plunged it toward his chest. Kalen was at my side, pushing me behind him as he shouted. Tanner's entire body jolted, and his eyes flared wide with pain. It took me a second to realize that the hand that had slammed into his chest had been the one holding the cuff blade.

I stumbled back in shock, knocking into the bed. "What...?"

"I'm sorry." Tanner's voice came out as a whisper. His eyes closed, and then he just...sucked into himself, folding from the top of his salt and pepper hair to the polished loafers on his feet. He crumpled like paper. There was a crack, a sound like a muffled gunshot, then a flash of intense light.

Then...nothing.

All that was left where Tanner once stood was the iron blade, remaining where it had fallen.

Chapter 18

I sat on the bed while Kalen called…well, I don't know who he called. In situations like these, he normally would've called Tanner, and I doubted he'd call Faye when she was dealing with her cousin.

But he spoke to someone while I sat there, holding the iron cuff and staring at the spot where Tanner had been standing.

I was still angry, but I was also…I just couldn't believe that Tanner had sent himself back to the Otherworld. Whatever Caden or I would've done to him would've paled in comparison to what would happen to him in a realm ruled by the Winter Queen. We would've killed him. End of story. But a fae stabbed by iron didn't die. It basically sent them home, and being sent to the Otherworld was a fate worse than death.

Not that he didn't deserve it, but I…

I just couldn't believe any of this.

"Brighton."

Blinking, I realized that Kalen had been speaking to me. "I'm sorry?"

"It's all right. I said…" He dragged a hand through his hair, trailing off as he stared at the same spot as I did. "I can't believe this. I wouldn't have believed any of this if I hadn't seen it with my own eyes."

"I thought that maybe he'd told Tatiana and perhaps her brother. So that they'd know what was happening and she could pursue Caden, you know?" I explained hoarsely, running my fingers over the cuff. "I had no idea."

"I don't know what to even say." Kalen turned away from the spot. "I really don't."

"Neither do I."

It was only a few minutes later that Caden filled the doorway. I looked up, my heart seizing at the sight of him. The urge to race over to him hit me hard. I was starting to stand when I realized what I was doing and stopped myself. Was he still mad at me? Well, obviously, he had to be. One didn't get over all that he learned in a matter of hours. I wasn't sure if he would want me to go to him, to touch him.

And God, that was another sting on an already raw, rapidly spreading wound.

Caden had halted, but then he was striding forward, coming to where I sat. I half expected him to stop there or to put space between us.

That's not what he did.

He knelt, gently taking my face in his hands. The contact was a jolt to the system as his gaze searched mine. "Are you okay?"

I started to answer, but his touch threw me for a loop, and all my hesitation slipped away.

Dropping the cuff onto the bed, I all but launched myself at Caden. If he were unprepared, he didn't show it. He caught me in his arms and straightened, holding me tightly. He didn't push me away. I buried my face in his chest, inhaling deeply. That didn't mean that everything was peachy and perfect between us, but I needed him—needed to feel him, to smell him, to be held by him—and he was here.

That meant everything.

"Brighton?" he murmured, smoothing a hand through my hair and down my back as I felt his head turn. "Is she okay?"

"Physically, yes," came Kalen's answer.

"I'm fine." My voice was muffled and probably barely coherent, but I didn't lift my head. "I'm just...it was Tanner, Caden. It was *him.*"

Tension strummed through every part of his body as he said to Kalen, "Tell me what you know."

Kalen did exactly that, but he didn't know everything. I did. Forcing myself to put it together, I lifted my head and reluctantly stepped back. I told Caden everything Tanner had told me, and he went from tense to downright rigid when I got to the part about Aric.

I was pacing by that point, one arm curled over my stomach. "He kept saying that he thought he was doing the right thing—"

"He wasn't," growled Caden.

"I know." I stopped, meeting his gaze. "I was going to kill him. I trusted him. My mom trusted him. *You* trusted him. But I was going to kill him." Tearing my gaze from Caden's hard one, I started walking again. "That's when he grabbed the blade with a napkin and told me that Neal had left the city, but that he had to know that I was your weakness, and that Neal would've told others. He then told me—" I cleared my throat. "He told me that I needed to do what he'd failed to do. Protect the Court by never letting my guard down. And then he…"

"He sent himself back to the Otherworld," Kalen picked up where I left off. "What will be done to him there will… It will make whatever we could do to him here look like nothing."

A muscle worked along Caden's jaw. "That knowledge doesn't ease me. I want to watch the life seep out of his eyes."

Kalen didn't object to that.

Neither did I.

"Can you please sit?" Caden asked, and I stopped. "You should be resting, and nothing about any of this is restful." He turned to Kalen. "Can you get Luce? I want Brighton checked."

"Of course." Kalen bowed and then turned to leave.

I sat because he was right. I felt okay, but none of this was exactly stress-free.

"Are you sure you're okay?" Caden asked.

"I feel all right. He didn't try to hurt me." I pressed my lips together. "At least not this time. Are you okay?"

Caden stared at me. "You don't need to worry if I'm okay."

"But I do," I told him. "He said you were with Faye, handling Benji, and I know you trusted Tanner. Everybody trusted him."

"I'm worried about you and the baby right now—"

"And I'm worried about you," I cut in. "Those things aren't mutually exclusive."

His head tilted and, for a moment, I wondered if he was going to say anything. "I trusted Tanner as much as I trusted anyone. I never would have expected him to be behind this."

"I still can't believe it." I picked up the cuff, turning it over in my hands. "I should be relieved that at least we know who was responsible, but I can't feel that. I don't understand how he thought this was the right thing."

"Fear."

I looked up at Caden.

"Fear is what made him think it was right." He approached slowly, sitting beside me. "Some of the fae here have limited their contact with the outside world so much that the Winter fae and their Queen have become like…what do you call it? The thing that scares children?"

"Bogeymen?"

"Yes. That." He turned his head to me. "It's not that I don't think they're not a threat. They are, but fear and panic are far more dangerous than any creature out there. It's the only reason I can think of that would've caused him to take this path. His fear of the Court weakening was far greater than his fear of what I would do to him." His gaze dropped to the cuff. "Maybe some would say that I should make myself into something greater to fear, but my father didn't rule that way. Neither will I."

"I'm glad to hear that." I stopped turning the cuff. "Making people fear you only works for so long. We humans have a long, sordid history of doing that and failing, and..." I peeked up at him. "And that's not you. I mean, you're badass and can be very scary at times, but you're also kind. I never would have..."

"What?"

I lifted my gaze to his. "I wouldn't have fallen in love with you if you were the type to believe that fear is a tool to be used to rule people." I turned my attention back to the cuff, quickly changing the subject. "I can't imagine how people are going to react."

"This is going to hit everyone hard. Tanner was well-respected. He was cared for. Loved. Trusted," he said, exhaling roughly. "I could lie. I could swear Kalen to silence. But lies...they never work out as one intends, even when they're told with the best of intentions."

"No." My shoulders sank. "They don't. He...he said that he thought he was doing the right thing, just like we thought we were doing the right thing."

"He's wrong. What he did is nothing like our situation, Brighton. Not at all."

"I know. It's not the same, but I get the sentiment. You thought it was best to give me time before you told me everything. I thought it was best to push you away and keep the pregnancy a secret so everyone was safe. Neither of us was right. It's still not the same. I know that." I leaned over, placing the cuff on the end table. "But I...I keep seeing his face. He knew what he'd done was wrong. I think he even knew when he told Aric I was important to you, but he kept doing it anyway. And I know a lot has happened. God. Things won't stop happening, but I..." I looked up at him as something occurred to me—something important and powerful. "I don't want to keep messing up and making the wrong choices. I love you, Caden. I want this baby. I want us to be together. I don't know if I'll make a good Queen. Honestly, I'll probably suck at it, but I don't care. I want to be *your* Queen. I know you're mad at me—"

"I'm not mad at you, Brighton."

"Really? You sure you don't want to rethink that answer?"

His eyes met mine once more. "I don't need to think about it. I'm not mad. Even when I'm furious with something you've done, I'm never angry at you."

That sounded like it would be good, if a bit confusing, but I had a feeling that whatever he was going to say next might be worse.

"I'm disappointed," he said, and my shoulders drooped. I was right. That was worse. "I—"

Whatever he was about to say was cut off by Luce's arrival. My blood pressure was a little high, which wasn't exactly surprising. And then others arrived, one after another. Faye. Tink. Fabian. Ren and Ivy. Some fae I recognized but didn't know their names. Others I wasn't sure I'd seen before.

There was a lot of disbelief. Not a single person or fae who came through the door could believe or understand why Tanner had done what he did. There were long moments of shocked silence, there were tears, and then Caden reassured everyone that life at Hotel Good Fae would continue, and that things would be rough, but that it would be okay. And as I sat there, listening to how calm he was, how sure he sounded, I didn't doubt for one second that things would eventually be okay once enough time had passed to move past the shock of Tanner's betrayal and the grief of his loss that was still to come, no matter what he'd done.

I didn't think I realized until then that Caden had truly been born to be a leader. I think he even eased Ren's and Ivy's concern, which was truly saying something. They left to share the news with Miles.

The whole time, Caden remained at my side. I kept expecting him to leave. I imagined that he needed to make a statement to all the fae at one time, but he didn't go.

There wasn't much for me to do as I sat there, other than to replay what'd happened with Tanner over and over and also wonder what it would take for Caden to no longer be disappointed.

If that was even possible.

I had to believe that it was. Like Hotel Good Fae, it would take time. There would be grief. There would be anger, but we had to get past this.

We had to.

Eventually, only Fabian and Tink remained in the room with us. Tink was standing in the corner, leaning against the wall. He'd been quiet through most of this, and I worried about him. He really liked Tanner, and I knew this had to be hitting him hard.

"There is something I can do," Fabian said after he and Caden discussed what needed to be done and whether what Tanner had said about Neal could be believed. Like me, I didn't think there was a reason to doubt what Tanner had claimed. Neal wasn't a problem. For now, at least. "I know you'll need to speak with the Court, but Tink and I can hold things down here while you make sure Brighton and my future niece or nephew actually get some stress-free rest."

I opened my mouth.

"We got this." Tink pushed off the wall, joining Fabian. "Consider these early godfather duties."

I closed my mouth as Caden frowned at the whole godfather thing. I fully expected him to thank them for the offer but pass. He was King, after all.

"Thank you. I appreciate it," Caden said.

Slowly, I turned toward him. "But aren't you needed? Don't you have to talk to them?"

"I'm needed here more," he said.

Too afraid to hope that was a positive sign, all I could do was nod. Tink came to my side, then bent and kissed my cheek. "Please get some rest."

"I will," I promised, catching his arm as he pulled away. "Are you okay?"

He gave me a small, sad smile. "I will be."

"It's a lot."

"It is." He slipped free, and then he left with Fabian.

The door closed behind them, and then I was alone with Caden, sitting close but not touching. I was exhausted, but I knew I wouldn't be sleeping anytime soon. There was too much going on in my head and—

"Tanner was wrong," Caden stated, pulling me out of my thoughts.

"I think there are a lot of things he was wrong about."

"Yes, but there was something he was very wrong about." He looked over at me then. "You're not my weakness."

My lips parted on a sharp inhale.

His gaze searched mine. "I could sense that you expected me to leave."

"I...I did. I imagined that they'd want to see you. You're really good at calming others."

"They will want to see me, and they will. But like I said, I'm needed here. I know you're tired. I can sense that too, but there's something I need to finish telling you."

Heart rate picking up, I nodded.

"I *was* disappointed, Brighton. I tried to clarify that, but we got interrupted. We keep getting interrupted," he said. "It seems like that's a trend for us."

"Yes," I whispered. "It is."

He lowered his chin, leaning in so that our faces were only a few inches apart. "I was disappointed and overwhelmed. Of all the ways I'd thought to find out I was going to be a father, this wasn't one of them. It was a lot to process, but what you said earlier? About not wanting to keep making the wrong choices? I agree. What Tanner did is nothing like us, but we both thought we were doing the right thing. I should've told you. You should've told me. We both messed up."

I felt like I couldn't breathe again, but this time for an entirely different reason. "We did."

"I think we're going to mess up again, sunshine," he said, and my breath caught at the use of my nickname. "It's bound to happen, especially since we're going to be raising a child. I imagine we're going to mess up a lot with that, too, but you know what that doesn't change, right?"

I nodded. "That…that we love each other?"

"Right." He took my face in his hands. "You hold a part of my soul, Brighton. You are my everything. Nothing will change that. Ever."

A strangled sound left me as I grasped the front of his shirt. "I love you."

We moved at the same time, and the moment our lips touched, it was like taking the first deep breath of summer air. The kiss was sweet and somehow more powerful than any we'd shared before. Maybe because it was the first kiss we'd shared with nothing hidden between us. Perhaps because it felt like a beginning.

Ending the kiss, he rested his forehead against mine as he slid a hand down my arm, to the curve of my hip and then to my lower stomach. "We are going to have a baby."

I smiled widely, blinking back tears—happy ones as I placed my hand over his. "We are."

"I haven't even thought about having a child, sunshine. But from the moment I learned that you were pregnant, even with everything going on, I knew in that moment that I wanted to be a father."

"I know the feeling." I squeezed his hand. "It was a shock, but I knew immediately that I wanted this child."

"You'll be a great mother."

"You think so?"

He pulled back so he could see my face. "I know so. Why would you doubt that?"

"I…I haven't had any more hallucinations or…breaks in reality. But that doesn't mean I won't. And I know you think it will be different for me, but I can't help but worry. I want to give this child what I didn't have. I want to be a mother who is always there, and what if…what if I'm not?"

He touched my cheek again. "We have no idea what tomorrow holds, but I can promise you that you're not alone. If you have more moments or not, I'm here. You have me. Our child will have both of us, no matter what, and we've got enough love already for this child that it will be enough. We will give him or her everything they could ever need." He kissed my forehead. "Besides, I have a feeling this kid is going to be strong. They'll be able to handle anything."

I shuddered. "Luce thinks that the child is already strong-willed and determined to live."

Caden folded his arms around me, gathering me close. "I don't doubt that for one second, not when it's you who's carrying this child. I don't know anyone, human or fae, more strong-willed and determined to live than you."

I lifted my head, kissing him again, and for the first time in my life, I felt no fear, no anger, and no worry.

Both of us had gone through our own hell to get here. We deserved it. Our child deserved it. All I felt was love.

I was whole.

Epilogue

Caden

Lounging on the plush grass of the enclosed courtyard outside of Hotel Good Fae, I watched my baby girl toddle after Tink. The brownie was, well, brownie-sized at the moment, his translucent wings nearly invisible in the bright, warm sunlight as he zipped up and then dipped down, staying just out of reach of Scorcha's chubby little fingers. She laughed and shrieked, attempting to jump in hopes of catching Tink, who taunted her by sticking out his tongue and tugging on a half-undone pigtail. With her blond hair and her mother's eyes, she was a bouncing beam of sunlight.

Scorcha.

My damn heart felt like a fist had taken hold of it and squeezed. Naming our daughter after my sister had been all Brighton's idea, one that had surprised me, but I'd wholeheartedly supported it the moment I got over the shock. The thoughtfulness behind the gesture still choked me up and didn't stop amazing me.

I shifted my gaze to the woman behind my baby girl. Every time I saw her, it happened. Every damn time. There was a hitch in my throat, and a sense of wholeness that never failed to render me utterly dumbstruck.

Brighton's hair was loosely braided, and several golden strands had slipped free, resting against her cheek and the slope of her neck as she caught Scorcha as she stumbled back in her hundredth attempt to catch Tink. Laughing at whatever Tink said to her, Brighton made sure that Scorcha was as stable as possible on her feet and then let go.

Brighton had been worried about what kind of mother she'd be, and I'd been right when I'd told her that I had no doubt she'd be absolutely wonderful. She knew exactly when to catch our daughter and when to let her go.

My gaze swept over her hungrily. Since the temps were expected to rise, she'd donned a gauzy, deep blue dress this morning. One with those silly, little straps I wanted to follow with my fingers, my tongue, and then my teeth. They drove me crazy, especially when they slipped off her shoulders—like now. A bolt of pure, complete, and absolute lust pounded through me. The corner of my lips tipped up as I watched the breeze lift and ruffle the panels of the dress, playing peekaboo with her legs. It reminded me of this morning when I woke, starving for her, and saw the curve of one exposed thigh. Her flesh had looked oh so lonely, peeking out from between the sheets, and I'd been more than happy to reintroduce the lovely expanse of skin to my hand and then my lips. I'd reached the junction of her thighs by the time she woke.

She was the best breakfast I'd ever eaten.

Hell. I could practically taste her on the tip of my tongue right now.

I shifted on the ground, giving myself a little extra room as I counted down the hours to Scorcha's afternoon nap. I was very, *very* hungry again.

Seeming to sense my damn near obsessive perusal, Brighton looked over at me. Our gazes connected as I ran the tip of my tongue over my upper lip. Pink flushed her cheeks as she shook her head at me, but I scented the sharp rise of arousal. It reminded me of roses drenched in vanilla, and it was addicting.

At least once a day I found myself wondering how in any world I had gotten so damn lucky. And there were still times when I couldn't shake the feeling that I wasn't worthy of her, our daughter, and the life we were building together, the future that was waiting for us. My time under the spell of the Winter Queen still followed me into my sleep and invaded the most hidden corners of my mind, but Brighton always found me in those moments. Whether at night, where she chased the nightmares away with sweet kisses, or when I fell into sullen silences and she was there to pull me from the grasp of the darkness. Just like I was there when the nightmare of Aric found her. I always reminded her that she was safe. I'd been right about the breaks in reality. She never had another one, but even if she had, we'd be okay.

We'd be more than okay.

Scorcha let out a squeal of triumph when she caught Tink's leg. I winced in sympathy. My baby girl had one hell of a grip. Just the other day, she'd grabbed my nose for whatever reason, and I'd thought she was going to yank it right off my face. And considering that with each passing day, her fae strength grew, it seemed plausible.

Tink only laughed and shouted, "You win! You win!"

Letting go of his leg, she clapped happily. "Again! Again!"

Swooping down, Tink kissed the crown of blond hair and then darted out of her reach. "You won't catch me again."

"Nuh-uh!" Scorcha did her funny little jerky knee run after Tink that was stopped by a loud, lioness yawn.

"I think she's going to end up sleeping through the afternoon once it's her naptime." Brighton tucked a strand of hair back from her face. "I may end up right with her."

Not if I had anything to do with that. I planned to make good use of our alone time.

The brownie glanced over at me as his wings beat furiously. "You're welcome."

I chuckled. "I owe you one."

Tink zipped up, narrowly avoiding Scorcha's grasp as Brighton's gaze met mine again. I read the unspoken message and nodded in agreement. We really would owe Tink for today. Since he and my brother had taken over the management of Hotel Good Fae, both were busy, and I didn't think anyone was more surprised than Tink by his dedication to continuing the success of the safe harbor for the fae.

"This is great practice, though," said Tink. "Since I plan on being the Mary Poppins of brownies."

"That reminds me. Have Ren and Ivy decided on a name yet?" Brighton asked.

"No," he answered. "They're still arguing between two names, and neither will listen to any of my suggestions."

"Did you suggest they name their son after you?" she asked.

"I did, but you want to know a secret?" Tink hovered far above Scorcha's head. "I gave them a whole list of names, and one of them was my actual name. They have no idea."

Brighton's mouth dropped open.

Shaking my head, I wondered if I should ruin Tink's day by telling Brighton what his actual name was. But as Brighton attempted to guess what it was, and her eyes narrowed in fond annoyance, I decided that piece of information could be shared at another time.

Glancing over my shoulder at the hotel, it was almost hard to believe just how well Hotel Good Fae was running these days. Things had been a mess after Tanner's betrayal, with half of the Court considering leaving. If it hadn't been for Tink and Fabian, I'd have grave concerns about the future of the sanctuary.

Recently, Ren had suggested that we may be experiencing a welcomed lull in the war against the Winter fae, but the truth was, the war for mankind hadn't really started.

The hotel was invaluable to the survival of the Summer Court. Not just because there were so many expecting females now, who were about to usher in the next generation, or the fact that nearly every room was filled. But because the threat of the Winter fae was still very much a concern, one that would not fade anytime soon.

There were still more Winter fae than Summer. If anything, their attacks had become more violent, commonplace, and senseless. With Aric's death and the disappearance of Neal, they lacked any true leadership, which was far more dangerous. Numerous Winter fae were doing their best to prove that they were more than capable of stepping up, and that led to even more deaths. Then there was the Devil's Breath, capable of turning any fae into a monster that needed to be dealt with. Just last week, a youngling had turned and had to be put down. Neal's disappearance only slowed the supply of the toxic drink. He was still out there, as was the Devil's Breath, but finally, the Order was working alongside the fae to discover the source of the supply. There were still Ancients, who I was sure, at this very moment, were plotting how to free Queen Morgana.

And then there was Queen Morgana herself.

While trapped in the Otherworld, she wasn't exactly the most pressing concern, but she was still alive, and I knew she was still attempting to find a way to open the gateway between the Otherworld and this one. Eventually, she would find a way, and that was when the real war would begin, one that would rapidly spread throughout the human world, involving them whether they liked it or not.

But that war wouldn't start today.

Focusing on the here and now, I exhaled slowly, heavily. Content despite what we may one day face, I refused to borrow from tomorrow's problems. No one could live like that.

Not even a King.

So, I watched what was most important to me. Right here, a handful of feet away, was my entire world.

Well, minus the brownie.

Although, his babysitting skills were incomparable.

But Scorcha would one day grow older, no longer just our little princess but the Princess of the Summer Court, and she would become as fierce and brave as her mother. She would be a fighter. The hand that now clutched her mother's would one day be just as confident holding an iron dagger, clutched in a gloved fist. That, I would make sure of.

And Brighton was...she was and always would be my *mortuus*—the most beautiful, courageous, strong, clever and kind woman I'd ever known. How much she meant to me could never have been seen as a weakness, and it never would be again. I wouldn't allow it. If anyone ever tried to use her or our daughter to control or manipulate me, it would be the very last thing they ever did. And it wasn't just me who would ensure that. I pitied the imbecile who thought Brighton an easy target. She'd always had claws, but with the birth of Scorcha, those claws had sharpened into deadly points. A smile tugged at my lips as Scorcha almost caught Tink once more. Brighton could take care of herself and then some, but if she needed backup, she had me.

She always had me.

Hours later, once Scorcha had fallen asleep and we were finally alone, I stripped Brighton bare and showed her just how beautiful I thought those faded scars were. I worshiped them with my lips and then my tongue, and always with my soul. I kissed her on the mouth and then lower, driving her to the peak of release over and over until my name was a prayer on her lips. Then, and only then, did I roll her onto her side and slide into her hot, tight depths.

"Fuck," I groaned, dropping my cheek to hers. I held myself still as long as I could, until the urge to move became almost painful. "I need you."

She knew exactly what that meant. "You have me."

I did.

Shuddering, I gripped her by the hip and lifted her onto her knees. For a moment, I was a little lost in the graceful slope of her back and the rounded, plump ass. She was beautiful. Always. I curled my arms around her shoulders, holding her in place as I took what she gave me.

Love.

Acceptance.

Understanding.

Strength.

There was no more slow buildup. No more time to play. I moved against her hard, slamming into her, driven by her soft moans filling the room and how she didn't just take each thrust but met them, riding me just as fiercely as I took her. She felt too damn good. My blood pounded, and I lost all semblance of control the moment I felt her clench and spasm around my dick. It was like losing my mind as I thrust into her, over and over until release found me. It was like lightning streaking down my spine, obliterating my senses. Hell if I knew how we'd ended up on our sides, her in front of me, my front to her back.

"I love you," she said, letting her head fall against my chest.

I smiled against her flushed skin and then kissed her shoulder. "You are my sun. My strength. My redemption. My heart. My everything. My Queen. I will always love you."

* * * *

Also from 1001 Dark Nights and Jennifer L. Armentrout, discover The Prince, The King, From Blood and Ash, A Kingdom of Flesh and Fire, and Dream of You.

Sign up for the 1001 Dark Nights Newsletter
and be entered to win a Tiffany Key necklace.

There's a contest every month!

Go to www.1001DarkNights.com to subscribe.

**As a bonus, all subscribers can download
FIVE FREE exclusive books!**

Discover 1001 Dark Nights Collection Seven

Visit www.1001DarkNights.com for more information.

THE BISHOP by Skye Warren
A Tanglewood Novella

TAKEN WITH YOU by Carrie Ann Ryan
A Fractured Connections Novella

DRAGON LOST by Donna Grant
A Dark Kings Novella

SEXY LOVE by Carly Phillips
A Sexy Series Novella

PROVOKE by Rachel Van Dyken
A Seaside Pictures Novella

RAFE by Sawyer Bennett
An Arizona Vengeance Novella

THE NAUGHTY PRINCESS by Claire Contreras
A Sexy Royals Novella

THE GRAVEYARD SHIFT by Darynda Jones
A Charley Davidson Novella

CHARMED by Lexi Blake
A Masters and Mercenaries Novella

SACRIFICE OF DARKNESS by Alexandra Ivy
A Guardians of Eternity Novella

THE QUEEN by Jen Armentrout
A Wicked Novella

BEGIN AGAIN by Jennifer Probst
A Stay Novella

VIXEN by Rebecca Zanetti
A Dark Protectors/Rebels Novella

SLASH by Laurelin Paige
A Slay Series Novella

THE DEAD HEAT OF SUMMER by Heather Graham
A Krewe of Hunters Novella

WILD FIRE by Kristen Ashley
A Chaos Novella

MORE THAN PROTECT YOU by Shayla Black
A More Than Words Novella

LOVE SONG by Kylie Scott
A Stage Dive Novella

CHERISH ME by J. Kenner
A Stark Ever After Novella

SHINE WITH ME by Kristen Proby
A With Me in Seattle Novella

And new from Blue Box Press:

TEASE ME by J. Kenner
A Stark International Novel

FROM BLOOD AND ASH by Jennifer L. Armentrout
A Blood and Ash Novel

QUEEN MOVE by Kennedy Ryan

THE HOUSE OF LONG AGO by Steve Berry and MJ Rose
A Cassiopeia Vitt Adventure

THE BUTTERFLY ROOM by Lucinda Riley

Discover More Jennifer L. Armentrout

From Blood and Ash
A Blood and Ash Novel
Now available

Captivating and action-packed, From Blood and Ash is a sexy, addictive, and unexpected fantasy perfect for fans of Sarah J. Maas and Laura Thalassa.

A Maiden…
Chosen from birth to usher in a new era, Poppy's life has never been her own. The life of the Maiden is solitary. Never to be touched. Never to be looked upon. Never to be spoken to. Never to experience pleasure. Waiting for the day of her Ascension, she would rather be with the guards, fighting back the evil that took her family, than preparing to be found worthy by the gods. But the choice has never been hers.

A Duty…
The entire kingdom's future rests on Poppy's shoulders, something she's not even quite sure she wants for herself. Because a Maiden has a heart. And a soul. And longing. And when Hawke, a golden-eyed guard honor bound to ensure her Ascension, enters her life, destiny and duty become tangled with desire and need. He incites her anger, makes her question everything she believes in, and tempts her with the forbidden.

A Kingdom…
Forsaken by the gods and feared by mortals, a fallen kingdom is rising once more, determined to take back what they believe is theirs through violence and vengeance. And as the shadow of those cursed draws closer, the line between what is forbidden and what is right becomes blurred. Poppy is not only on the verge of losing her heart and being found unworthy by the gods, but also her life when every blood-soaked thread that holds her world together begins to unravel.

* * * *

A Kingdom of Flesh and Fire
A Blood and Ash Novel
Coming September 1, 2020

From #1 *New York Times* bestselling author Jennifer L. Armentrout comes a new novel in her Blood and Ash series…

Is Love Stronger Than Vengeance?

A Betrayal…

Everything Poppy has ever believed in is a lie, including the man she was falling in love with. Thrust among those who see her as a symbol of a monstrous kingdom, she barely knows who she is without the veil of the Maiden. But what she *does* know is that nothing is as dangerous to her as *him*. The Dark One. The Prince of Atlantia. He wants her to fight him, and that's one order she's more than happy to obey. *He may have taken her, but he will never have her.*

A Choice….

Casteel Da'Neer is known by many names and many faces. His lies are as seductive as his touch. His truths as sensual as his bite. Poppy knows better than to trust him. He needs her alive, healthy, and whole to achieve his goals. But he's the only way for her to get what she wants—to find her brother Ian and see for herself if he has become a soulless Ascended. Working with Casteel instead of against him presents its own risks. He still tempts her with every breath, offering up all she's ever wanted. Casteel has plans for her. Ones that could expose her to unimaginable pleasure and unfathomable pain. Plans that will force her to look beyond everything she thought she knew about herself—about him. Plans that could bind their lives together in unexpected ways that neither kingdom is prepared for. And she's far too reckless, too hungry, to resist the temptation.

A Secret…

But unrest has grown in Atlantia as they await the return of their Prince. Whispers of war have become stronger, and Poppy is at the very heart of it all. The King wants to use her to send a message. The Descenters want her dead. The wolven are growing more unpredictable. And as her abilities to feel pain and emotion begin to grow and strengthen, the Atlantians start to fear her. Dark secrets are at play, ones steeped in the blood-drenched sins of two kingdoms that would do anything to keep the truth hidden. But when the earth begins to shake, and the skies start to bleed, it may already be too late.

* * * *

The Prince: A Wicked Novella

She's everything he wants….
Cold. Heartless. Deadly. Whispers of his name alone bring fear to fae and mortals alike. *The Prince.* There is nothing in the mortal world more dangerous than him. Haunted by a past he couldn't control, all Caden desires is revenge against those who'd wronged him, trapping him in never-ending nightmare. And there is one person he knows can help him.

She's everything he can't have…
Raised within the Order, Brighton Jussier knows just how dangerous the Prince is, reformed or not. She'd seen firsthand what atrocities he could be capable of. The last thing she wants to do is help him, but he leaves her little choice. Forced to work alongside him, she begins to see the man under the bitter ice. Yearning for him feels like the definition of insanity, but there's no denying the heat in his touch and the wicked promise is his stare.

She's everything he'll take….
But there's someone out there who wants to return the Prince to his former self. A walking, breathing nightmare that is hell bent on destroying the world and everyone close to him. The last thing either of them needs is a distraction, but with the attraction growing between them each now, the one thing he wants more than anything may be the one thing that will be his undoing.

She's everything he'd die for….

* * * *

The King: A Wicked Novella

From #1 *New York Times* and *USA Today* bestselling author Jennifer L. Armentrout comes the next installment in her Wicked series.

As Caden and Brighton's attraction grows despite the odds stacked against a happily ever after, they must work together to stop an Ancient fae from releasing the Queen, who wants nothing more than to see Caden become the evil Prince once feared by fae and mortals alike.

* * * *

Dream of You: A Wait For You Novella

Abby Erickson isn't looking for a one-night stand, a relationship, or anything that involves any one-on-one time, but when she witnesses a shocking crime, she's thrust into the hands of the sexiest man she's ever seen - Colton Anders. His job is to protect her, but with every look, every touch, and every simmering kiss, she's in danger of not only losing her life but her heart also.

From Blood and Ash
A Blood and Ash Novel
By Jennifer L. Armentrout

Captivating and action-packed, From Blood and Ash is a sexy, addictive, and unexpected fantasy perfect for fans of Sarah J. Maas and Laura Thalassa.

A Maiden…

Chosen from birth to usher in a new era, Poppy's life has never been her own. The life of the Maiden is solitary. Never to be touched. Never to be looked upon. Never to be spoken to. Never to experience pleasure. Waiting for the day of her Ascension, she would rather be with the guards, fighting back the evil that took her family, than preparing to be found worthy by the gods. But the choice has never been hers.

A Duty…

The entire kingdom's future rests on Poppy's shoulders, something she's not even quite sure she wants for herself. Because a Maiden has a heart. And a soul. And longing. And when Hawke, a golden-eyed guard honor bound to ensure her Ascension, enters her life, destiny and duty become tangled with desire and need. He incites her anger, makes her question everything she believes in, and tempts her with the forbidden.

A Kingdom…

Forsaken by the gods and feared by mortals, a fallen kingdom is rising once more, determined to take back what they believe is theirs through violence and vengeance. And as the shadow of those cursed draws closer, the line between what is forbidden and what is right becomes blurred. Poppy is not only on the verge of losing her heart and being found unworthy by the gods, but also her life when every blood-soaked thread that holds her world together begins to unravel.

* * * *

"They found Finley this eve, just outside the Blood Forest, dead."
I looked up from my cards and across the crimson-painted surface to

the three men sitting at the table. I'd chosen this spot for a reason. I'd…felt nothing from them as I drifted between the crowded tables earlier.

No pain, physical or emotional.

Normally, I didn't prod to see if someone was in pain. Doing so without reason felt incredibly invasive, but in crowds, it was difficult to control just how much I allowed myself to feel. There was always someone whose pain cut so deeply, was so raw, that their anguish became a palpable entity I didn't even have to open my senses to feel—that I couldn't ignore and walk away from. They projected their agony onto the world around them.

I was forbidden to do anything but ignore. To never speak of the gift bestowed upon me by the gods and to never, ever go beyond sensing to actually doing something about it.

Not that I always did what I was supposed to do.

Obviously.

But these men were fine when I reached out with my senses to avoid those in great pain, which was surprising, given what they did for a living. They were guards from the Rise—the mountainous wall constructed from the limestone and iron mined from the Elysium Peaks. Ever since the War of Two Kings ended four centuries ago, the Rise had enclosed all of Masadonia, and every city in the Kingdom of Solis was protected by a Rise. Smaller versions surrounded villages and training posts, the farming communities, and other sparsely populated towns.

What the guards saw on a regular basis, what they had to do, often left them in anguish, rather it be from injuries or from what went deeper than torn skin and bruised bones.

Tonight, they weren't just absent of anguish, but also their armor and uniforms. Instead, they donned loose shirts and buckskin breeches. Still, I knew, even off duty, they were watchful for signs of the dreaded mist and the horror that came with it, and for those who worked against the future of the kingdom. They were still armed to the teeth.

As was I.

Hidden beneath the folds of the cloak and the thin gown I wore underneath, the cool hilt of a dagger that never quite warmed to my skin was sheathed against my thigh. Gifted to me on my sixteenth birthday, it wasn't the only weapon I'd acquired or the deadliest, but it was my favorite. The handle was fashioned from the bones of a long-extinct wolven—a creature that had been neither man nor beast but both—and the blade made of bloodstone honed to fatal sharpness.

I may yet again be in the process of doing something incredibly reckless, inappropriate, and wholly forbidden, but I wasn't foolish enough to enter a place like the Red Pearl without protection, the skill to employ it, and the wherewithal to take that weapon and skill and use them without hesitation.

"Dead?" the other guard said, a younger one with brown hair and a soft face. I thought his name might be Airrick, and he couldn't be much older than my eighteen years. "He wasn't just dead. Finley was drained of blood, his flesh chewed up like wild dogs had a go at him, and then torn to pieces."

My cards blurred as tiny balls of ice formed in the pit of my stomach. Wild dogs didn't do that. Not to mention, there weren't any wild dogs near the Blood Forest, the only place in the world where the trees bled, staining the bark and the leaves a deep crimson. There were rumors of other animals, overly large rodents and scavengers that preyed upon the corpses of those who lingered too long in the forest.

"And you know what that means," Airrick went on. "They must be near. An attack will—"

"Not sure this is the right conversation to be having," an older guard cut in. I knew of him. Phillips Rathi. He'd been on the Rise for years, which was nearly unheard of. Guards didn't have long lifespans. He nodded in my direction. "You're in the presence of a lady."

A lady?

Only the Ascended were called Ladies, but I also wasn't someone anyone, especially those in this building, would expect to be inside the Red Pearl. If I was discovered, I would be in…well, more trouble than I'd ever been in before and would face severe reprimand.

The kind of punishment that Dorian Teerman, the Duke of Masadonia, would just love to deliver. And which, of course, his close confidante, Lord Brandole Mazeen, would love to be in attendance for.

Anxiety surfaced as I looked at the dark-skinned guard. There was no way Phillips could know who I was. The top half of my face was covered by the white domino mask I'd found discarded in the Queen's Gardens ages ago, and I wore a plain robin's egg blue cloak I'd, uh, *borrowed* from Britta, one of the many castle servants who I'd overheard speaking about the Red Pearl. Hopefully, Britta wouldn't discover her missing overcoat before I returned it in the morn.

Even without the mask, though, I could count on one hand how many people in Masadonia had seen my face, and none of them would be here tonight.

As the Maiden, the Chosen, a veil usually covered my face and hair at all times, all except for my lips and jaw.

I doubted Phillips could recognize me solely on those features, and if he had, none of them would still be sitting here. I would be in the process of being dragged back, albeit gently, to my guardians, the Duke and Duchess of Masadonia.

There was no reason to panic.

Forcing the muscles along my shoulders and neck to ease, I smiled. "I'm no Lady. You're more than welcome to talk about whatever you wish."

"Be that as it may, a little less morbid topic would be welcomed," Phillips replied, sending a pointed look in the direction of the other two guards.

Airrick lifted his gaze to mine. "My apologies."

"Apologies not needed but accepted."

The third guard ducked his chin, studiously staring at his cards as he repeated the same. His cheeks had pinkened, something I found rather adorable. The guards who worked the Rise went through vicious training, becoming skilled in all manner of weaponry and hand-to-hand combat. None who survived their first venture outside the Rise came back without shedding blood and seeing death.

And yet, this man blushed.

I cleared my throat, wanting to ask more about who Finley was, whether he was a guard from the Rise or a Huntsman, a division of the army that ferried communication between the cities and escorted travelers and goods. They spent half the year outside the protection of the Rise. It was by far one of the most dangerous of all occupations, so they never traveled alone. Some never returned.

Unfortunately, a few who did, didn't come back the same. They returned with rampantly spreading death snapping at their heels.

Cursed.

Sensing that Phillips would silence any further conversation, I didn't voice any of the questions dancing on the tip of my tongue. If others had been with him and had been wounded by what most likely had killed Finley, I would find out one way or another.

I just hoped it wasn't through screams of terror.

The people of Masadonia had no real idea exactly how many returned from outside the Rise cursed. They only saw a handful here and there, and not the reality. If they did, panic and fear were sure to ignite a populace who truly had no concept of the horror outside the Rise.

Not like my brother Ian and I did.

Which was why when the topic at the table switched to more mundane things, I struggled to will the ice coating my insides to thaw. Countless lives were given and taken by the endeavor to keep those inside the Rise safe, but it was failing—had been failing—not just here, but throughout the Kingdom of Solis.

Death....

Death *always* found a way in.

Stop, I ordered myself as the general sense of unease threatened to swell. Tonight wasn't about all the things I was aware of that I probably shouldn't be. Tonight was about living, about...not being up all night, unable to sleep, alone and feeling like...like I had no control, no...no idea of who I was other than *what* I was.

Another poor hand was dealt, and I'd played enough cards with Ian to know there was no recovering from the ones I held. When I announced that I was out, the guards nodded as I rose, each bidding me a good evening.

Moving between the tables, I took the flute of champagne offered by a server with a gloved hand and tried to recapture the feelings of excitement that had buzzed through my veins as I'd hurried through the streets earlier that evening.

I minded my business as I scanned the room, keeping my senses to myself. Even outside of those who managed to project their anguish into the air around them, I didn't need to touch someone to know if they were hurting. I just needed to see someone and focus. What they looked like didn't change if they were experiencing some sort of pain, and their appearance didn't change when I concentrated on them. I simply *felt* their anguish.

Physical pain was almost always hot, but the kind that couldn't be seen?

It was almost always cold.

Bawdy shouts and whistles snapped me out of my own mind. A woman in red sat on the edge of the table next to the one I'd left. She wore a gown made of scraps of red satin and gauze that barely covered her thighs. One of the men grabbed a fistful of the diaphanous little skirt.

Smacking his hand away with a saucy grin, she lay back, her body forming a sensual curve. Her thick, blonde curls spilled across forgotten coins and chips. "Who wants to win me tonight?" Her voice was deep and smoky as she slid her hands along the waist of the frilly corset. "I can assure you boys, I will last longer than any pot of gold will."

"And what if it's a tie?" one of the men asked, the fine cut of his coat suggesting that he was a well-to-do merchant or businessman of some sort.

"Then it will be a far more entertaining night for me," she said, drawing one hand down her stomach, slipping even lower to between her—

Cheeks heating, I quickly looked away as I took a sip of the bubbly champagne. My gaze found its way to the dazzling glow of a rose-gold chandelier. The Red Pearl must be doing well, and the owners well connected. Electricity was expensive and heavily controlled by the Royal Court. It made me wonder who some of their clientele was for the luxury to be available.

Under the chandelier, another card game was in progress. There were women there too, their hair twisted in elaborate updos adorned with crystals, and their clothing far less daring than the women who worked here. Their gowns were vibrant shades of purple and yellow and pastel hues of blue and lilac.

I was only allowed to wear white, whether I was in my room or in public, which wasn't often. So, I was fascinated with how the different colors complemented the wearer's skin or hair. I imagined I looked like a ghost most days, roaming the halls of Castle Teerman in white.

These women also wore domino masks that covered half their faces, protecting their identities. I wondered who some of them were. Daring wives left alone one too many times? Young women who hadn't married or were perhaps widowed? Servants or women who worked in the city, out for the evening? Were Ladies and Lords in Wait among the masked females at the table and among the crowd? Did they come here for the same reasons I did?

Boredom? Curiosity?

Loneliness?

If so, then we were more alike than I realized, even though they were second daughters and sons, given to the Royal Court upon their thirteenth birthday during the annual Rite. And I...I was Penellaphe of Castle Teerman, Kin of the Balfours, and the Queen's favorite.

I was *the* Maiden.

About Jennifer L. Armentrout

1 New York Times and International Bestselling author Jennifer lives in Shepherdstown, West Virginia. All the rumors you've heard about her state aren't true. When she's not hard at work writing, she spends her time reading, watching really bad zombie movies, and hanging out with her husband, a crazy Border Jack puppy named Apollo, six judgmental alpacas, five fluffy sheep, and two goats.

Her dreams of becoming an author started in algebra class, where she spent most of her time writing short stories...which explains her dismal grades in math. Jennifer writes young adult paranormal, science fiction, fantasy, and contemporary romance. She is published with Tor Teen, Entangled Teen and Brazen, Disney/Hyperion and Harlequin Teen. Her book *Wicked* has been optioned by Passionflix and slated to begin filming in late 2020. Her young adult romantic suspense novel *DON'T LOOK BACK* was a 2014 nominated Best in Young Adult Fiction by YALSA and her novel *THE PROBLEM WITH FOREVER* is a 2017 RITA Award winning novel, and her novel *STORM AND FURY* was chosen for the 2020-2021 Florida Teens Read List.

She also writes Adult and New Adult contemporary and paranormal romance under the name J. Lynn. She is published by Entangled Brazen and HarperCollins.

Discover 1001 Dark Nights

Visit www.1001DarkNights.com for more information.

COLLECTION ONE
FOREVER WICKED by Shayla Black
CRIMSON TWILIGHT by Heather Graham
CAPTURED IN SURRENDER by Liliana Hart
SILENT BITE: A SCANGUARDS WEDDING by Tina Folsom
DUNGEON GAMES by Lexi Blake
AZAGOTH by Larissa Ione
NEED YOU NOW by Lisa Renee Jones
SHOW ME, BABY by Cherise Sinclair
ROPED IN by Lorelei James
TEMPTED BY MIDNIGHT by Lara Adrian
THE FLAME by Christopher Rice
CARESS OF DARKNESS by Julie Kenner

COLLECTION TWO
WICKED WOLF by Carrie Ann Ryan
WHEN IRISH EYES ARE HAUNTING by Heather Graham
EASY WITH YOU by Kristen Proby
MASTER OF FREEDOM by Cherise Sinclair
CARESS OF PLEASURE by Julie Kenner
ADORED by Lexi Blake
HADES by Larissa Ione
RAVAGED by Elisabeth Naughton
DREAM OF YOU by Jennifer L. Armentrout
STRIPPED DOWN by Lorelei James
RAGE/KILLIAN by Alexandra Ivy/Laura Wright
DRAGON KING by Donna Grant
PURE WICKED by Shayla Black
HARD AS STEEL by Laura Kaye
STROKE OF MIDNIGHT by Lara Adrian
ALL HALLOWS EVE by Heather Graham
KISS THE FLAME by Christopher Rice
DARING HER LOVE by Melissa Foster
TEASED by Rebecca Zanetti
THE PROMISE OF SURRENDER by Liliana Hart

COLLECTION THREE
HIDDEN INK by Carrie Ann Ryan
BLOOD ON THE BAYOU by Heather Graham
SEARCHING FOR MINE by Jennifer Probst
DANCE OF DESIRE by Christopher Rice
ROUGH RHYTHM by Tessa Bailey
DEVOTED by Lexi Blake
Z by Larissa Ione
FALLING UNDER YOU by Laurelin Paige
EASY FOR KEEPS by Kristen Proby
UNCHAINED by Elisabeth Naughton
HARD TO SERVE by Laura Kaye
DRAGON FEVER by Donna Grant
KAYDEN/SIMON by Alexandra Ivy/Laura Wright
STRUNG UP by Lorelei James
MIDNIGHT UNTAMED by Lara Adrian
TRICKED by Rebecca Zanetti
DIRTY WICKED by Shayla Black
THE ONLY ONE by Lauren Blakely
SWEET SURRENDER by Liliana Hart

COLLECTION FOUR
ROCK CHICK REAWAKENING by Kristen Ashley
ADORING INK by Carrie Ann Ryan
SWEET RIVALRY by K. Bromberg
SHADE'S LADY by Joanna Wylde
RAZR by Larissa Ione
ARRANGED by Lexi Blake
TANGLED by Rebecca Zanetti
HOLD ME by J. Kenner
SOMEHOW, SOME WAY by Jennifer Probst
TOO CLOSE TO CALL by Tessa Bailey
HUNTED by Elisabeth Naughton
EYES ON YOU by Laura Kaye
BLADE by Alexandra Ivy/Laura Wright
DRAGON BURN by Donna Grant
TRIPPED OUT by Lorelei James
STUD FINDER by Lauren Blakely
MIDNIGHT UNLEASHED by Lara Adrian

HALLOW BE THE HAUNT by Heather Graham
DIRTY FILTHY FIX by Laurelin Paige
THE BED MATE by Kendall Ryan
NIGHT GAMES by CD Reiss
NO RESERVATIONS by Kristen Proby
DAWN OF SURRENDER by Liliana Hart

COLLECTION FIVE
BLAZE ERUPTING by Rebecca Zanetti
ROUGH RIDE by Kristen Ashley
HAWKYN by Larissa Ione
RIDE DIRTY by Laura Kaye
ROME'S CHANCE by Joanna Wylde
THE MARRIAGE ARRANGEMENT by Jennifer Probst
SURRENDER by Elisabeth Naughton
INKED NIGHTS by Carrie Ann Ryan
ENVY by Rachel Van Dyken
PROTECTED by Lexi Blake
THE PRINCE by Jennifer L. Armentrout
PLEASE ME by J. Kenner
WOUND TIGHT by Lorelei James
STRONG by Kylie Scott
DRAGON NIGHT by Donna Grant
TEMPTING BROOKE by Kristen Proby
HAUNTED BE THE HOLIDAYS by Heather Graham
CONTROL by K. Bromberg
HUNKY HEARTBREAKER by Kendall Ryan
THE DARKEST CAPTIVE by Gena Showalter

COLLECTION SIX
DRAGON CLAIMED by Donna Grant
ASHES TO INK by Carrie Ann Ryan
ENSNARED by Elisabeth Naughton
EVERMORE by Corinne Michaels
VENGEANCE by Rebecca Zanetti
ELI'S TRIUMPH by Joanna Wylde
CIPHER by Larissa Ione
RESCUING MACIE by Susan Stoker
ENCHANTED by Lexi Blake

TAKE THE BRIDE by Carly Phillips
INDULGE ME by J. Kenner
THE KING by Jennifer L. Armentrout
QUIET MAN by Kristen Ashley
ABANDON by Rachel Van Dyken
THE OPEN DOOR by Laurelin Paige
CLOSER by Kylie Scott
SOMETHING JUST LIKE THIS by Jennifer Probst
BLOOD NIGHT by Heather Graham
TWIST OF FATE by Jill Shalvis
MORE THAN PLEASURE YOU by Shayla Black
WONDER WITH ME by Kristen Proby
THE DARKEST ASSASSIN by Gena Showalter

Discover Blue Box Press

TAME ME by J. Kenner
TEMPT ME by J. Kenner
DAMIEN by J. Kenner
TEASE ME by J. Kenner
REAPER by Larissa Ione
THE SURRENDER GATE by Christopher Rice
SERVICING THE TARGET by Cherise Sinclair
THE LAKE OF LEARNING by Steve Berry and MJ Rose
THE MUSEUM OF MYSTERIES by Steve Berry and MJ Rose

On Behalf of 1001 Dark Nights,

Liz Berry, M.J. Rose, and Jillian Stein would like to thank ~

Steve Berry
Doug Scofield
Benjamin Stein
Kim Guidroz
Social Butterfly PR
Asha Hossain
Chris Graham
Chelle Olson
Kasi Alexander
Jessica Johns
Dylan Stockton
Richard Blake
and Simon Lipskar

Made in the USA
Middletown, DE
15 October 2023

40636287R00102